Boy Oh Boy

stories

ZACHARY DOSS

Red Hen Press | *Pasadena, CA*

This book is the Winner of the 2019 Grace Paley Prize in Short Fiction. AWP is a national, nonprofit organization dedicated to serving American letters, writers, and programs of writing. AWP's headquerters are at Riverdale Park, Maryland.

Book design by Mark E. Cull

Library of Congress Cataloging-in-Publication Data

Names: Doss, Zachary, author.
Title: Boy oh boy : stories / Zachary Doss.
Description: First edition. | Pasadena, CA : Red Hen Press, 2020.
Identifiers: LCCN 2019041449 (print) | LCCN 2019041450 (ebook) | ISBN 9781597098137 (trade paperback) | ISBN 9781597098120 (ebook)
Classification: LCC PS3604.O827 A6 2020 (print) | LCC PS3604.O827 (ebook) | DDC 813/.6—dc23
LC record available at https://lccn.loc.gov/2019041449

The National Endowment for the Arts, the Los Angeles County Arts Commission, the Ahmanson Foundation, the Dwight Stuart Youth Fund, the Max Factor Family Foundation, the Pasadena Tournament of Roses Foundation, the Pasadena Arts & Culture Commission and the City of Pasadena Cultural Affairs Division, the City of Los Angeles Department of Cultural Affairs, the Audrey & Sydney Irmas Charitable Foundation, the Kinder Morgan Foundation, the Meta & George Rosenberg Foundation, the Allergan Foundation, the Riordan Foundation, Amazon Literary Partnership, and the Mara W. Breech Foundation partially support Red Hen Press.

First Edition
Published by Red Hen Press
www.redhen.org

Acknowledgments

Stories in this collection have appeared, sometimes in different versions or with different titles, in the following publications:

CHEAP POP, "Responsible Ownership"; *Entropy*, "Jane Eyre"; *Fourteen Hills*, "What Keeps Society Going"; *Heavy Feather Review*, "One Word for It," "The Natural Man"; *Hobart* (online), "How the Day Goes VIII"; *Juked* (online), "Cold Fish," "Trash Pope," "Trolling"; *Lockjaw Magazine*, "Spatial Awareness"; *Lumina*, "Fuck Marry Kill"; *Passages North* (online), "The Blood Mouth"; *The Mondegreen*, "How the Day Goes," "How the Day Goes II," "How the Day Goes III," "How the Day Goes IV"; *Monkeybicycle*, "Spy vs. Spy"; *New South* (online), "Godzilla," "Pest Control"; *Puerto del Sol* (online), "Bespoke"; *SmokeLong Quarterly*, "The Village with All of the Boyfriends"; *Sonora Review*, "Sadland"; *Wigleaf*, "You Could Fucking Sell That," "The Purses"; *Sundog Lit*, "Embodied," "Esquire," "Put a Ring on It"; *THIS.*, "Fraternal," "Higher Learning," "Sex Stuff," and "The Problem-Solver."

Contents

I

Your Boyfriend Always
Has Something He Wants to Do

Trolling 13

Cold Fish 15

Godzilla 17

Pest Control 19

Trash Pope 21

The Natural Man 23

Embodied 26

One Word for It 28

Put a Ring on It 31

On the Outside 33

II

And Then He Asks,
What Would You Do Differently?

How the Day Goes I 39

How the Day Goes II 40

How the Day Goes III 41

How the Day Goes IV 42

How the Day Goes V 43

How the Day Goes VI 44

How the Day Goes VII 45

How the Day Goes VIII 46

How the Day Goes IX 47

How the Day Goes X 48

III

I Am Having a Very Authentic Experience,
You Think

Bespoke 51

IV

You Love it All so Goddamn Much

Esquire 75
Sex Stuff 77
Fraternal 79
The Problem-Solver 81
Higher Learning 84

V

You Did the Things
That Made Sense to You

You Could Fucking Sell That 89
Spatial Awareness 93
Washington, Adams, Jefferson, Madison 97
The Purses 101
Transubstantiation 104
Sadland 107
Jane Eyre 113
Bump in the Night 115
Responsible Ownership 117
The Blood Mouth 119

VI

The Game Begins to Occupy
a Very Central Place in Your Life

Zombie Apocalypse Story 131
Manure 135
What Keeps Society Going 137
Spy vs. Spy 144
Fuck Marry Kill 150

VII

Boyfriends All the Way Down

Universal Boyfriend Theory 161

VIII

You Are Waiting
for a Foundation to Crack

The Village with All of the Boyfriends 189

I

*Your Boyfriend Always
Has Something He Wants to Do*

Trolling

WHEN YOU KEEP finding troll dolls around your apartment, you assume your boyfriend is playing a practical joke. You think your boyfriend is funny, like that time he asked you for ten dollars and then didn't contact you for six months after you gave it to him. The first troll has blue hair and a jewel in its belly and sits on top of your alarm clock. The second you find floating face down in your toilet tank. Its wet purple hair radiates from its head like a nerve.

You don't mention the trolls to your boyfriend. You pay for dinner and he talks about his job. This is part of the joke, you think, and you know the joke can go on for up to six months. When you open your bedroom door and the room is so full of troll dolls that they avalanche into the hallway, this is part of the joke. The joke is when you find, well, it must be half a million troll dolls, buried neck deep in your front lawn. Your first instinct is to call someone, but who? A gardener? A toy store?

The last straw is when there are no troll dolls at all, for a week and then longer, a month or two. You and your boyfriend start getting into fights. You don't bring up the troll dolls, but you yell about other things, about the time he left the butter out overnight. Your boyfriend yells back that you don't actually need to refrigerate butter, it will be fine. You're pretty sure you read that somewhere but you aren't willing to give any ground now.

Six months later, he calls, no reason, just wants to talk. You're pretty sure he wants something, but it feels good to hear him laugh. You open the junk drawer, but you don't remember what you were looking for when he called. He's talking about getting a new job. You find the first troll, blue hair with the belly jewel. What was the deal with the troll dolls, anyway? you ask, cutting him off.

I have no idea what you're talking about, he says, and now he's lost his place and has to start his story over.

Cold Fish

YOU'RE READY TO go home but your boyfriend is still floating on the lake, so far out he looks like a discarded T-shirt. You wave to get his attention, and when he doesn't look up, you think he might be dead. Eventually, though, he swims to shore and tells you to go home, he's going to stay here for a while.

You assume this is just a phase and go home. But he refuses to leave the lake. You keep going back, hoping he will change his mind. You bring him sandwiches and he eats them in the water, soggy bread and all. You carry a freshly laundered towel and try to lure him to shore with it.

When you drive away you watch him from your rearview mirror. He still looks dead to you, a spot of color floating in the dark water. Alone every night, you try not to worry. You think of things that could happen. Poisonous snakes. Man-eating fish. Water bears. Crocodiles. Jet skis.

You call your boyfriend's mother and explain your concerns. What is a water bear? she asks. You start to explain that it's a bear that lives in the water, and she hangs up.

Increasingly you become distracted at work and your performance suffers. You find yourself screaming at the dog, slamming the door on girl scouts.

This is becoming a problem, you say to him on your next visit.

You sit, your feet dangling in the cold water. Your boyfriend's lips and fingers are turning blue. He tugs on your big toe and you jump, thinking a fish is trying to pull you under.

I'm not coming back here, you say.

Your boyfriend splashes his face, pours water down his cheeks. Look, he says, it's just like I'm crying.

Godzilla

YOUR BOYFRIEND DECIDES to start a small business and sure enough the store he opens only comes up to your knee. Somehow he fits inside but as much as you scrunch you can't get in. Outside, on your hands and knees, you peek with one eye through the small windows.

When you ask him who his intended customers are, he says, Just really small people, I guess.

Through the window you can see your boyfriend industriously filling wicker baskets with scented soaps, making neat rows of colorful bubble bath bottles.

His shop is a disproportionately large success. Small people line up around the block for his honeysuckle-scented body lotion. He is interviewed by the local news. On television, he and his shop and the newscaster look like they are the correct size.

This won't change anything about our relationship, your boyfriend says.

You begin to fit uncomfortably into your own life. You ask coworkers, do I seem especially gigantic to you today? and while they assure you that you are normal-sized, they submit hostile work environment claims to the director of human resources.

After an argument you tell your boyfriend that you hate your job and think you are about to get fired. I can support us both, he says.

That isn't the point, you say.

Every day, as you walk by your boyfriend's shop, you imagine crushing the mob of tiny people waiting their turn to fill their tiny baskets with tiny fancy bath products, the little dark smears on the sidewalk, the way they would make the bottom of your boot sticky, the puffs of honeysuckle or lilac or rose scent on the air as you crush their bath products. You imagine biting their tiny heads off, drinking from their bleeding necks. You are big enough, and thirsty.

Pest Control

YOUR BOYFRIEND INVITES you to move in with him, but he lives inside a mechanical bull and you dread spending the night there. That would be a less than ideal living arrangement, you explain.

I hardly even notice the cowboys anymore, he says.

But really the cowboys are a nuisance. You turn on the kitchen light at night and cowboys skitter across the floor in their Wrangler jeans, their spurs clinking. When you try to fall asleep, you hear the cowboys crawling around in the dust under the bed, singing prairie songs around a campfire.

I'll call the landlord, your boyfriend says, but his landlord is busy running the country-western bar and he tells your boyfriend that there is a reason the rent for his mechanical bull is so low.

I don't deal with cowboy infestations or motion sickness, the landlord says.

Your boyfriend asks if you will dress as a cowboy during sex, says it might help you get more comfortable in the apartment. You try to ease into it by wearing a bandana and a pair of boots but then you remember that time you left the butter out and came back to tiny boot prints in it, and you can't keep an erection.

What if you moved? you ask your boyfriend. The truth is, you know your boyfriend doesn't mind the cowboys. He tries to tell you how cute they are if you look at them right, and how they help keep other pests out with their small guns, but to you they all look like they've rolled around in the gunk underneath the refrigerator.

I'm just saying, there must be apartments that don't have a cowboy problem, you say.

This is a very difficult real estate market, your boyfriend says. And it is, it really is.

Trash Pope

YOUR BOYFRIEND WANTS to become the Pope but there is already a Pope. Your boyfriend doesn't want to wait for the Pope to get sick or die or retire in disgrace, and decides he's going to be the Trash Pope instead.

Your boyfriend the Trash Pope goes out to live in the landfill outside of town. It's about as gross as you expect, but your boyfriend is optimistic. He nails two boards together for a cross and hangs it on a shack he builds out of discarded sheet metal.

Initially there is some trouble because your boyfriend has never read the Bible and has only the vaguest idea of what Catholics do. He doesn't speak Latin, so he tries Pig Latin instead. He burns the discarded stubs of candles. He blesses pools of stinking, rotten water.

I'm not sure what you're going for here, you say to your boyfriend the Trash Pope.

He finds a lot of dead bodies abandoned in the muck. He consecrates the remains and buries them behind his cathedral. He tries to fancy the cathedral up a little bit but it's still a metal shed draped with stained cloth with some broken wind chimes dangling off of it.

I don't remember there being a lot of wind chimes, you try to explain. You grew up Catholic but your boyfriend doesn't listen to your advice.

I'm the one who's Trash Pope, he says.

You start going to regular, non-trash church. It's comforting how clean the stained glass is, how bright the light on Sunday morning. Incense smells nicer than garbage, you say to the priest at confession.

You don't know how to explain this to your boyfriend. Everything here is so much nicer, it's enough that you just believe.

The Natural Man

YOUR BOYFRIEND DECIDES to grow his hair out. He has always kept himself carefully groomed, but lately he had been going to greater and greater lengths to manage hair growth. He waxes, he trims, he clippers, he tweezes. He keeps every follicle under such careful control that when he says he's going to grow it all out, just not worry about it for a while, you aren't surprised at how desperate he sounds, how lonely. You've always been a more natural kind of guy, but he knew that when you started dating.

At first, there is only a slight shagginess that you find appealing. It's boyish and interesting. It's something to grab on to, as you say when you thread your fingers through his hair during sex. You return to his hair frequently, ruffling it as you pass by or brushing it off his forehead when you kiss him. This is okay, you think, this is nice. Of course the hair on his body grows more slowly, so for the first several weeks you don't even notice that. You notice that his eyebrows seem less painstakingly arranged, less cultivated.

Soon, every surface of his body is bristly with new hair. He's uncomfortable to hug or fuck. When you kiss, it feels like you are kissing more beard than lip. The floor is covered with his hair. You have to sweep frequently. Otherwise, hair sticks to the bottom of your feet when you get out of the shower. When you have to pull the hairs off your feet, there is an uncomfortable tug, like you are pulling the hairs out of your skin.

As your boyfriend's hair proliferates, you drop hints about getting rug burn when you sleep too close to him, or always finding small hairs between your teeth, or even finding hair in your food. He ignores you while his hair grows even longer. He develops a thick, shaggy coat all over his body. You realize you never knew how much exactly he had to shave, how much waxing he must have done. You wonder what you were doing while your boyfriend was performing this maintenance. It must have taken hours.

One day, after a reluctant kiss, you notice that your boyfriend has grown fangs. Did he always have fangs? You are reasonably sure he didn't, but there he is, with oversized, pointed canines. He must have been filing them down all this time, you think. You search your bathroom for the tools, for files and clippers that might have been used to make teeth look straight and even and very normal. Then he grows long, craggy claws. And then he can't talk through his new, oversized teeth, so he barks or grunts. The more strange-looking your boyfriend becomes, the more normal-looking you remember him, until you remember him being perfect. Surely he had to have been perfect to become this deeply imperfect.

You view the inevitable damage to your relationship as his fault, not yours. You start to sleep on the couch, when you sleep at home. Usually you are out all night. You go to parties where everyone wears only underwear, and you admire the waxed chests and hairless backs. Eventually, you start hooking up. It seems an inevitable progression. You still appreciate a hairless asshole every once in a while. It seems like your boyfriend knows what you're getting up to. You come home in the early morning to find ruined furniture, chewed-up shoes, and sometimes he has peed or shit on the floor. When you leave, he stands at the door and whines, his eyes big, trying to express how much he is going to miss you.

Eventually, you buy a collar and a chain and start tying him up in the backyard. You stop telling the men you have sex with that you can't bring them home. You might as well, you think, as your boyfriend barks and scratches at the door. He howls as you bury your face in every hairless inch of every man you can find. It's such a relief. Eventually, you find a man you bring home a few times. Then he's over for dinner, to watch a movie, to nap and read on your couch. Your boyfriend barks and barks. He comes inside sometimes, but you tell the man who is not your boyfriend that your boyfriend is more of an outdoor pet. Out of guilt, you build your boyfriend a little house back there, but he refuses to live in it. He looks at you scornfully. He looks at the man who is not your boyfriend scornfully. He looks at the little house scornfully. He doesn't come to the door as often.

I think your dog hates me, the man who is not your boyfriend says.

Yeah, you say.

Embodied

YOUR BOYFRIEND IS leasing space inside your body. The rent you charge is reasonable, a steal really, but since you're in a relationship, you decide you're not going to push it by asking for what living space in your veins and between your organs is really worth. Your boyfriend comes and goes as he pleases through a slit in your back, parallel to your spine.

Sometimes, during the day, you feel a kind of heat on the inside of your skin, and you know that he's sitting or lying there, right inside your body, and you touch or stroke the spot to let him know you know he's there. He's very considerate, keeps the volume down on his television, makes sure everything is clean and well maintained. You've been breathing a little bit better lately, your heartbeat less erratic, and you know your boyfriend has been lovingly scrubbing your lungs and arteries, polishing each surface clean and gleaming, like he has removed decades of soot from a dirty window.

When you ask him to meet you for dates, he emerges from the slit parallel to your spine and he is covered in your blood and the other viscous fluids of your body. His hair is matted to his head and his hand is too slippery to hold. He shivers a little bit when he's with you, like being outside your body brings on a chill, and you take pride in this evidence of the heat of your viscera.

When your boyfriend starts to cancel dates with you, or doesn't show up when you've made plans, you are worried. Any number of things might have happened, like he has found someone else, or he has taken ill, or he fell down in the tub. You know from the warmth and pressure building along your tibia that he is still inside you. When you call him on the phone to ask why you haven't seen him very much lately, he says that he sees you all the time. In fact, he says he sees the parts of you that you can't see, and from the inside, with the light shining through your skin, your body is a cathedral.

You don't have much to say to that; you find a needle and thread and sew yourself shut.

One Word for It

YOUR BOYFRIEND IS trying to learn how to un-name things. You don't take this pursuit any more seriously than his other diversions, but he devotes hours of study to the practice. He just got fired, and you think he wants to un-name the restaurant he worked for to fuck with his old boss. This is an awful lot of trouble to go to, you say.

It's not about that, he says.

His first few efforts are an awful lot of trouble. The first try involves strange-looking glyphs, a bucket of oranges, a homeless black dog, and a knife. It is extremely messy and at the end, neither of you can remember what those things are called. You know, those things that are like cupcakes but . . . not cupcakes? Immediately, it seems like un-naming is very irritating. The word for not-cupcakes vanishes from bakeries and signs and advertisements and people take to ordering frosting-less cupcakes or bread cupcakes or just making a little outline with their fingers. I'm not sure I'm in love with this as a hobby for you, you say to your boy-friend.

I'm sure I can get it right, he says.

Subsequent attempts are more successful, although mostly they create more confusion. You find yourself constantly trying to talk around things. You coin terms like lawn hair and glass fish cage and foot glove. Your boyfriend does eventually un-name the restaurant he worked for, but shows no sign of stopping. You try to convince him that he is just making it more difficult for people to exist in the world, but he's convinced that he is acting for the public good.

It's true the language has taken on a strange, almost Shakespearian complexity, and everything sounds lovelier this way, less precise but more emotional. Still, you are wholly unconvinced you want to live the rest of your life in an undergraduate creative writing exercise. Your aggravation manifests itself in a series of increasingly obtuse arguments. You can't quite say that he's doing it on purpose, but your boyfriend keeps taking away your ability to communicate, reducing your pool of available nouns. When the black dog corpses piling up behind the garage begin to smell, the only way you can articulate your outrage is by saying, Stop doing that thing you keep doing, it's not great.

You think he should understand but he doesn't, just shakes his head at you as if you are being deliberately obscure. You resort to inarticulate screaming, and to be completely honest, you are surprised by how deeply satisfying you find it. You scream, again and again, imbuing each scream with incredibly nuanced emotions you find it too frustrating to communicate in any other way.

He sits at the edge of your bed until you are finished screaming. I'm sorry, he says. I thought this would help. He says other things, things that sound lovely to you in the way that hearing someone speak Italian is lovely. It is impassioned and elegant garbage. When he's done, he looks at you pleadingly and you can only shake your head. You laugh uncomfortably because you don't understand. You attempt to reassure him, but it comes out as a startled bark.

He takes your hand in his and cradles it, rolling his thumb over the skin and bone. The un-naming starts with the pads of your fingers, the ridges of your fingertips, your knuckles, your skin, each sculpture of bone. He goes up your arm, your elbow, your shoulder, removing the name from each muscle group and vein and tissue cluster, each lump of cartilage. Freckles, hairs, moles, warts, tumors, he un-names. His finger traces your jaw until you do not know finger or jaw. He un-genders you, un-sexes you, smudges away the details of your face, any softness or hardness you may once have had is now unspeakable. He whispers your name gently and then that goes too, he peels it off you and you are naked and what remains is beautiful and beyond description.

Put a Ring on It

You buy your boyfriend a ring, a simple affair, plain silver band. On the inside is engraved, I am my beloved's and my beloved is mine. You've been getting all the right signals from him for a while. One morning, you wake up and he has surrounded your bed with a circle of salt. He seems alarmed when you cross it, easily, to kiss him good morning.

Later, as he waves a burning hank of sage in your face, you are thinking about the ring, which is tucked inside a pair of underwear in your dresser. I've been thinking lately it might be time to talk about a long-term commitment, you say out loud. He chants back in Latin, his voice low and sonorous, something *Deo, protego* something, *omnis immundus spiritus*.

Come to bed, you say to him.

Adjuramus te, he says.

The ring was really more like an impulse buy, and you're a little concerned that maybe you aren't ready. But you've come to appreciate the little things he does for you. Most nights, you come home from work to a black goat, throat slit, its blood pooled in a wide, silver bowl beside your bed.

He plants a circle of vervain around the house you share. He carves runes into the lintels of the French doors.

You wait for exactly the right moment to take the ring out of your underwear drawer. The lighting is perfect; your boyfriend has filled the room with candles, and two priests are holding hands and chanting. The air shimmers with heat and the chanting has a dulling effect on the senses. Your boyfriend holds a silver dagger shaped like a cross and an ornate chalice filled with water.

Will you marry me? you ask.

He splashes you in the face with the water and presses the blade flat against your cheek hard enough that two thin lines of blood appear. His hand grips your neck below the jaw, holding your face still as he draws the knife down your cheekbone.

You know, you say, this only works if you believe in it.

On the Outside

YOUR BOYFRIEND WAS raised by sexy wolves. The sexy wolves live out on the edge of town, in beautiful open-plan lofts with real wood flooring and big floor-to-ceiling windows. The sexy wolves are super sexy, and they teach your boyfriend to be super sexy too. The sexy wolves go to the gym at least twice a day. The sexy wolves make chicken in big batches and portion it out for the week, six ounces at a time, and pair it with some vegetables. The sexy wolves do yoga class, Pilates class, water aerobics class, fencing class, tennis class, ballet class, CrossFit. The sexy wolves wear tank tops, crop tops, short-shorts, cute hats, colorful high-tops, tiny underwear that doesn't cover much. The sexy wolves get their bodies waxed, expensive haircuts, buy only the best moisturizers and hair products. The sexy wolves respect the whole package; they are educated, hard-working, talented. The sexy wolves have interesting and diverse hobbies that they pursue, are passionate about one or more charities, are well-versed in the arts. The sexy wolves know that kindness is sexy, confidence is sexy, intelligence is sexy, geekiness is sexy. They have big books where all the rules and laws related to being sexy are laid out.

You meet your boyfriend at a charity marathon. I like to combine my love of physical fitness with my love of charity, he says.

You are struck by how sexy your boyfriend is, just in the way he stands, the way he laughs, the way his eyes crinkle at the corners. He licks his bottom lip in a way that is conscious in that it seems so unconscious. Everything about him seems low-effort but very careful and intentional and expensive, like he just happened to wake up that morning wearing the best workout clothes, with the line of his jockstrap rising just slightly above his running shorts, his fitted shirt not quite covering a strip of exposed flesh.

After the race you ask for your boyfriend's phone number and he takes your phone from you and types it in himself, puts his name in with a little heart emoji and a little wink emoji. When he puts the phone back in your hand, his fingertips gently brush your wrist and somehow you swear you can smell him there for the rest of the day. You bring your wrist up to your nose almost inadvertently as you go about your business, at the grocery store, the laundromat, the taqueria where you meet your friends for margaritas. Your friends caution you about the sexy wolves who live out on the edge of town, but when you press them for details the discomfort is somehow impossible for them to articulate. They're just . . . too sexy, one of your friends says, twirling the stem of his margarita glass, which is shaped like a cactus, between three of his fingers.

Before bed, you text your boyfriend: I'm glad I met you.

He texts you a response: I'm glad I met you too ;)

You go on dates with your boyfriend and you're constantly on alert, should he be too sexy like your friend said.

It's true your boyfriend is a lot of different kinds of sexy. Sometimes he's movie sexy, like when he winks at you and says, you haven't seen anything yet, tiger. Other times he's a wholesome kind of sexy, in pastel-colored button-down shirts and aviators, and he looks like he could meet your mom on Easter. Sometimes he's jock sexy, in shirts with cut-off sleeves and workout shorts. Sometimes he's chill sexy, he is most often chill sexy, he is so incredibly chill, smokes cigars with the boys, drinks whiskey straight, laughs at dirty jokes and talks about sports he enjoys. But despite all that, he's never too sexy. You feel like he's exactly the right amount of sexy for you.

You aren't sexy at all, or you don't think you are. You've always been a little buttoned-up, straight-laced. Every Sunday you clean your apartment, top to bottom, and during the week you get the same sandwich from the same deli every day and when you watch TV, it's usually to watch a show that you already know you like. You are fit but doughy, not athletic-looking in the least. You like boring music, the kind they play on the radio all the time, and you went to a regular college and got middle-of-the-road grades and when you graduated, you got the regular kind of job that everyone has. When your boyfriend says, that's so interesting! about your job, you assume he is being insincere but it is very sexy that he seems so interested in what you do.

When you plan dates, your boyfriend always asks you what you want to do, and you always shrug and say, I don't know, anything really, what do you want to do?

Your boyfriend always has something he wants to do. He takes you with him to laser tag, black light bowling, mini golf, indoor rock climbing, underwear parties, underground raves, whiskey tastings, baseball games, operas. He gets you to try ecstasy and you participate in an orgy that you barely remember. You go scuba diving. He has connections at the zoo, and together you get a behind-the-scenes tour where you get to throw raw steaks to the lions, who regard you with an imperial indifference you feel down to your bones. He takes you with him to the bar where you watch reality shows with a big crowd and you have to take a drink every time someone on the TV says I'm not here to make friends. You get drunk, your boyfriend gets drunk, everyone is drunk.

While you are spending a lot of time with your boyfriend, you haven't met any of the sexy wolves. When you drive out to the edge of town, you see them, from a distance, dancing shirtless in the street, licking melted ice cream off each other's hands in the heat, but by the time you get close enough to see in greater detail, they're all gone, there's only your boyfriend, waiting for you on the sidewalk in a tight black t-shirt and jeans that are torn so that you can see part of his ass. When you ask him about his family, he just shrugs you off. I've never met my real family, he says, but the sexy wolves raised me. As you drive away, you can hear their sultry howling in the distance.

Is it very hard, being so sexy all the time? you ask your boyfriend.

It is, your boyfriend says, super hard.

II

And Then He Asks,
What Would You Do Differently?

How the Day Goes I

YOUR BOYFRIEND LISTENS to a lot of Fiona Apple, feels sad for no reason, lacks confidence in his writing. Your boyfriend won't get off fucking Twitter. To cheer him up you bring your boyfriend flowers and cupcakes and a small wooden doll. The small wooden doll is the kind where you can bend its limbs into different poses, the kind artists sometimes use for models, but a smaller version, small enough to fit in the palm of your hand. Your boyfriend twists the small wooden doll's limbs into a strange shape, a kind of dance. He sets the small wooden doll on one of the cupcakes, mooshes it down into the icing. Then he leaves the room and you spend some time looking at the doll dancing on top of the cupcake, trying to decide what it all means.

How the Day Goes II

YOUR BOYFRIEND IS having a hard time at his job. There are numerous difficulties, his boss, the grind of his daily tasks, the generally poor quality of the office equipment. It's depressing, he spends his whole day on social media. I come home every day tired from doing nothing, he says, and it's true, he has been especially tired lately. You tell him to quit, but he shrugs and asks what you would do for money if he quit. You are honest, tell him you don't know, which is maybe the wrong answer, but neither of you makes a lot of money. He talks about getting a better job, both of you getting better jobs, but neither of you can imagine being qualified to do anything better than what you're doing now. Together you go out to the lake where you spent much of your teen years, together you drink a case of beer and watch the sun rise over the water. You suggest wandering out into the hills, getting lost and never coming back. He shrugs. As a compromise, you leave your empty cans in the muddy lakebed, set end-to-end, spelling out HELP.

How the Day Goes III

YOU AND YOUR boyfriend go to a lot of funerals. Friends, friends of friends, relatives, people you both only barely knew from the office. Your favorite bartender dies. The bagger at the grocery store dies. The waitress who gives bad service at your favorite restaurant dies. You and your boyfriend go to all the funerals. It seems like you dry-clean your suit every week. The weather refuses to turn gloomy; it's unusually sunny and warm for spring, you sweat through your shirt every time you walk from the small stone church to the overfull graveyard. When the mailman dies, you stop getting invitations to the funerals because there's no one to deliver them. Instead people rely on social media. Social media will outlive all of us, your boyfriend says at one funeral. But soon after that, social media dies. You and your boyfriend agree to skip all future funerals, but later you catch him hanging out at the small stone church, wearing a freshly cleaned suit, waiting for the next funeral to start. You stay for that funeral, and the next one, but you'll be damned if you spend any more money dry-cleaning that suit.

How the Day Goes IV

YOUR BOYFRIEND GETS sick. It's not the kind of sickness where he will eventually recover. It's the kind of sickness in which you must make the most of the time you have left together, which is what everyone tells you. You are both unsure of how to make the most of the time you have left together. You take up team sports, go to cooking classes, learn to scrapbook, join a church, take a road trip. You expect the road trip to be emotionally fraught, but you're both pretty agreeable the whole time. In Arizona, you try a burger made out of emu, which you agree is gross. He kisses you on the cheek and you take a picture with a cactus. You ask him how sick he feels and he shrugs and says, not very. You don't feel very sick either. When you get back from your road trip, you're both out of things you wanted to do together, so you go back to your jobs. You made the most of the time you had left, but you didn't plan for any extra time. Thank God we don't have to scrapbook anymore, your boyfriend says. So dumb, you agree.

How the Day Goes V

WHEN YOU GET to the cake store, the cake man, in his pastel pink cake store uniform, is standing outside smoking a cigarette. You think he looks ridiculous but you can't tell what your boyfriend thinks anymore. As you approach the store and it becomes clear you might want to enter, the cake man shakes his head. Freezer's broken, he says, the cakes have all gone bad.

Couldn't you just make another cake, your boyfriend asks.

The man in the cake store uniform shrugs and takes a drag on his cigarette. He has long fingers, the tips of his index and middle fingers stained with tobacco where he holds the cigarette. From a distance, he seemed ridiculous, but up-close he is beautiful, you have to admit he is beautiful. The cake man says, Nobody makes anything anymore.

You shrug and your boyfriend shrugs and you both keep walking. You came all this way to get a cake for your anniversary but actually it makes sense to both of you that there wouldn't be a cake. Cakes have all gone bad, your boyfriend says, and you think he sounds thoughtful, but you still can't tell what he's thinking. Seems like, you say.

How the Day Goes VI

YOUR BOYFRIEND ASKS you to try holding the baby. You are aware that he is testing you, but you take the baby anyway, you hold the baby like someone who doesn't want to hold the baby. The baby smells like baby, which is to say like very fresh garbage, and his head is soft, visibly soft, like modeling clay. I could make this baby into anything, you think as you hold him. You should rock him gently, or coo, but you stand stiffly with your forearms positioned so the baby cannot possibly be comfortable. But the baby is so soft he just takes the shape of your arms, so it's your back that hurts from holding the baby this way and the baby is fine. Babies are always fine, you think, and you notice that the baby's mother is telling your boyfriend that babies are surprisingly resilient. They can survive anything, she says, and the way she says this is grim and terrifying. You want to hand the monster baby back to his mother, but what you do is blurt out, I didn't want this. Going forward, your relationship with the baby and his mother is unfriendly.

How the Day Goes VII

YOU AND YOUR boyfriend are talking about your dream jobs. You say that you want to be extremely wealthy, and he asks what job you want to do in order to become extremely wealthy. You hadn't thought about it that way before. You pick at the piping on the cushion of your secondhand couch from the '70s. It was your dead grandmother's couch, and it looks like a dead grandmother's couch. Your boyfriend asks you again about the job, the actual job, because you went to state college and got mediocre grades, and right now your actual, non-dream job involves selling golf balls, and your boyfriend points out that he doesn't really see a clear path to wealth for you now, and then he asks, what would you do differently? The question floats between you like something deadly, a poisonous insect maybe. You are both very quiet as you've realized what he actually said. One of you has to change the subject now, before it's too late. If a silence like that continues on for too long, it becomes impossible to get rid of.

How the Day Goes VIII

YOUR BOYFRIEND GETS a job at the Ghost Factory. He works the morning shift so he's usually gone before you wake up. After he is gone, the pillow smells like him but it's lukewarm, the same temperature as the air, the walls, your skin, and your breath. At the Ghost Factory, your boyfriend pulls a machete off a rack on the wall and by the time you wake up and heat a cup of tea, he is hacking the ghosts apart. He finds it satisfying, your boyfriend, the way the blade bites into joints. He tosses the ghost parts into bins marked for example 'legs' or 'arms' or 'torsos.' There is a bin marked 'scraps' for genitals and heads, the useless parts of a ghost. Your boyfriend is slick with blueblack gore up to his biceps. You can't drink your tea fast enough, the last half-inch always goes lukewarm, the temperature of the air, the sidewalk, the bus stop, your hands, and the tip of your tongue. You are waiting for the bus. Your boyfriend is staring into black eyes, carving ghosts into parts small enough to carry, or hide, or swallow.

How the Day Goes IX

YOU AND YOUR boyfriend purchase land on which you plan to build a home. The land is far away and located at a place so inconvenient to reach that you can't imagine living there until you have fewer obligations that require you to be in the city. For now, you rent a small apartment and go to your jobs and put away some of your paychecks to someday be able to build on your land. In the meantime, the land has been subject to some mishaps. Recently there was a flood. You hear about the flood on the news, you and your boyfriend climb in his pickup truck and drive to your land. There is a dirt road leading to the center, where you plan to build your home. However, the road is impassable; the center of your property has filled with water, a wide, low lake. The rain has cleared and the still water is a perfect reflection of the sky. You sit with your boyfriend on the bed of his truck. It is warm and humid because of the rain. Your home, you imagine, is somewhere in the middle of all that water.

How the Day Goes X

FINALLY, YOU AND your boyfriend decide everything is so fucking boring you're not even going to bother with it.

III

*I Am Having a Very Authentic Experience,
You Think*

Bespoke

YOU DECIDE TO order a new boyfriend. You don't exactly need a new boyfriend, not yet. Your old one is just fine. Sure, he's running a little hot these days, his fan whirs a little loudly, his memory a little slower than you would find on newer models. But in all the particulars, he's serviceable. You've had your boyfriend for five years, and he's been a good boyfriend. There for you when you need him. He dresses up nicely for work functions, where you take him to show off how handsome he is. He is nice to your mother. He likes to watch television exactly as much as you like to watch television, and you like all of the same shows.

You are a compulsive catalog shopper. You have been looking online, surreptitiously, sneaking glances at the newest models when your boyfriend is charging or while you're at work. On your work computer, you stream the conference where they announce the new boyfriends, slim and toned and shiny. An older fat man gestures towards the new boyfriends, a row of them, and they stand on the stage and smile. A blonde boyfriend waves. A boyfriend with dark skin gives a thumbs-up. The older fat man turns a tan boyfriend around and jiggles his butt with his palm. The crowd laughs. The tan boyfriend looks over his shoulder and grins. He has impossibly clean, white, even teeth. He looks like a Hardy Boy. He is the beach model, you think, checking a dog-eared page in the catalog. This is the boyfriend you've had your eye on.

A new boyfriend is thousands of dollars, but you have some money saved up. You look at the catalogs and the websites and the online reviews again and again. It's the slow season at your job, so you don't really have that much to do. You're earning your paycheck but not much in the way of commissions or bonuses. This time of year is exactly like that, slow. In your spare time, you convince yourself that eventually, you'll need to get a new boyfriend anyway. Every time your old boyfriend drops a plate in the sink and breaks it, bumps into a doorframe, forgets the word for traffic or tractor or cheese, spontaneously loses his charge when he is supposed to have 20% battery life left, you're reminded that really, it's only a matter of time.

You can't exactly live without a boyfriend. You've always had one to take care of you. You justify the thousands of dollars a boyfriend costs by reasoning that, really, they do a lot for you. You interact with your boyfriend fairly regularly, even if that just means fucking him a couple of times a day. You've always had an active sex drive. When you were a teenager, you masturbated four or five times a day. Once, on a Sunday, you got up to eleven times, an accomplishment you still remember with some measure of pride. The boyfriends are kind of a sex thing, although you've convinced yourself that they aren't really a sex thing. They are a thing you have sex with, sometimes, but they're more than that. Just like a real relationship.

You got your first boyfriend in college. He was on sale, nine hundred dollars, maybe nine hundred and fifty. A lot, for a college student, but even then you recognized a bargain and loved to save money. You remember the first boyfriend fondly. He was cheap, only lasted a little over a year and a half before his processor fried, but you had some good times. He was handsome. All the boyfriends are handsome, but this one had a crooked nose. The boyfriend designers thought introducing minor physical idiosyncrasies to the boyfriends might make them more attractive, not less, although that proved an unpopular design choice. You liked it, though. You looked at his crooked nose and believed in him.

That first boyfriend did everything you needed him to. He kept your apartment clean. He did dishes, although he wasn't great at it, and you often found plates with missed spots of caked-on food. He did a good enough job for a college student. He couldn't drink with you, or even fake it like newer models can, but he sat next to you while you smoked pot and he rubbed your thigh and told you the things you were saying were very smart. His speech recognition was bad, so sometimes he gave the wrong response to something you said, but you programmed him to call you Daddy in bed, something you found pretty funny at nineteen, and he could do that without screwing up most of the time.

The boyfriends aren't really a sex thing but they've always been best at putting out. Actually, they are marketed as friends and companions. In the commercials, they do light housework, they take notes at meetings, they mimic active listening, they make convincing small talk. They can wear suits at funerals and they can sit by the swimming pool on a sunny day without overheating too much and they can save your spot in a long line and they can go to a movie with you and offer their opinions, which are based on a synthesis of the top fifty most popular online reviews, which is to say, they have opinions that are objectively more correct than yours.

They do other things in the commercials too, like drive cars and cook meals and babysit and play tennis, but a disclaimer appears at the bottom of the screen in big white letters saying basically that the boyfriends can't do any of those things, or they can, but not very well, and you should not let the boyfriends operate heavy machinery and you should never, ever leave your children alone with a boyfriend and you eat their cooking at your own risk. They cannot, for example, tell the difference between salt and sugar and rat poison. They cannot really differentiate between your child and someone else's child or a medium-sized dog unless your child or the dog is microchipped.

But obviously you can fuck them too, they have all the correct parts for that, and the anatomy is so convincing you honestly can't tell the difference, and why would they make the boyfriends attractive and fuckable if they didn't want people to fuck them. They used to sell a non-fuckable variety that was so unpopular that almost nobody ever bought one. You've never seen one, although you heard rumors that parents would give them to teenagers as birthday presents, handsome and neutered chaperones. Now, they sell online for hundreds of thousands of dollars to obsessive collectors, the same people who collect dollar bills with printing errors or dolls made with three eyes instead of two or stamps printed upside-down.

The time you spend researching a replacement boyfriend makes you feel guilty about your current boyfriend. You have weathered difficult times together. He has been your boyfriend for what seems now to have been a very, very long time. It seems like longer the more you think about it. Sitting on the couch watching superhero TV shows together, the shows that he likes and you also like, you take his hand and say, We've weathered difficult times together, haven't we?

He pauses briefly before responding. We have, he says finally, weathered difficult times together.

It is comfortable to hear him say that. You imagine that the times were difficult for him as well as for you. You have imbued him with a life, with a backstory. You pretend he has a job. You pretend that he had difficulties in his life that were equal to the difficulties you had in your life. No, you go back and decide that maybe his difficulties could be a little bit less than yours. You like the idea that you got him through a hard time but the hard time you had was worse and you were still available to be his rock. You could have scripted these things and programmed them into your boyfriend's memory, so that you could talk him through his difficulties and he could be incredibly grateful to you, like you deserve, but you've never done that. His personality is the default personality. He is not at all distinctive. What passes for his persona is cobbled together from people in movies and people on TV shows and people in songs and people in romance novels. You don't care; to you, he is convincing. You don't want him to tell you things that you wrote for him to say. You would prefer to come as close as possible to not knowing the outcome, even though you know the outcome.

Tonight, for example, you know the outcome. The TV show you're watching comes to the end. You ask your boyfriend what he thinks will happen in the next episode, and in seconds, he has repeated a theory he found on a message board online that his programming has deemed most compelling. The pitch of his voice changes, and his speech speeds up so he sounds excited. He leans forward, his eyes widen. You try not to notice them individually, but you know there are a thousand tiny cues programmed into him to communicate interest, excitement, boyish charm.

Instead of thinking about that, you kiss him. You have not been with many real boys, real boyfriends with asymmetrical faces, too-large foreheads, gap teeth, but to you it seems like your boyfriend feels exactly the same. His skin is exactly correct, the right amount of give, the right temperature; his mouth still tastes like dinner even though he didn't eat any. When you press closer to him, he whimpers slightly, exactly as if he were surprised and aroused by your passion. I am having a very authentic experience, you think.

You and your boyfriend have always had fairly boring sex. People assume boyfriends are for weird stuff, a partner who is totally pliant and willing and discreet. You thought that too, you thought you would do weird stuff with your boyfriend, learn a new kind of sex that was extreme and perverse, but not really. Your boyfriend can be programmed to do just about anything, but you couldn't think of exactly what you would want him to do except the regular stuff. The defaults. You have watched videos of the other stuff online and it just made you feel uncomfortable. You didn't really want to program your boyfriend to do any of that. You don't really have the kind of imagination that would require. Sexually, you are very normal, you think. You are very average. You have an average body and an average dick and an average amount of passion. You have no STDs, or fetishes, or weird feelings about race, or special sexual tricks for which your ex-lovers might have remembered you. There is nothing overwhelmingly exciting about you, but there is nothing wrong with you.

There is nothing wrong with you. With your boyfriend, you perform admirably. You don't skimp on the foreplay, even though your boyfriend is already aroused, or as aroused as you want him to be. Even though his arousal is some secret switch inside of him that flips immediately and stays flipped. Even though you don't need him to be in the mood because he doesn't have moods to be in or out of. You wonder what he thinks about, if he's still compiling theories about the superhero TV show in some sub-process while he is also being fucked. You wonder if he is also compiling your routine for tomorrow, setting alarms so that he can gently wake you, stroking your forehead while he tells you what's coming up in the day ahead. You wonder if he is wirelessly reviewing the inventory of your refrigerator and making a grocery list. You wonder what he thinks about when he's alone.

Mid-moan, his eyes roll back in his head and you think, this is new, but you realize when his eyes close that he has simply shut down, his battery has lost its charge. You are still inside him, but you feel awkward suddenly, as if you had been caught doing something wrong. The heaters that kept your boyfriend's skin warm and lifelike cool quickly and his skin begins to feel strange, rubbery and cold. At this point, you have two options, you can finish, because you are very near completion anyway, or you can stop and pull out. You are considering this problem when you realize that you have gone almost completely soft, your problem is no longer a problem. Maybe you didn't feel like finishing anyway. You plug your boyfriend into the wall so he will charge, and as he's charging, he begins to generate heat again. His body is as warm as yours, maybe a little warmer, which makes it easy to fall asleep next to him.

At the boyfriend store, the only employee is an older fat man. He looks just like the older fat man you watched in the video of the conference, the man with the broad, chubby palm who jiggled the butt of the tan beach boyfriend. You swear it is the same man, but you also think, how strange that the CEO of this company also works at the retail locations. You go back and forth on this, trying to convince yourself that it is or isn't the same man. He watches you calmly, a pleasant expression on his face, as if he is waiting for you to resolve this train of thought before he says anything.

The boyfriend store is incredibly sleek, all metal and glass and white light and pale wood. It is a long, narrow store full of long, narrow tables, rectangles of light supported by wooden frames. They look like tables from some futuristic movie. The boyfriends lay on the tables, deactivated, their faces frozen in grins, their eyes fixed on some point at or past the ceiling. When they are active, the boyfriends look just like real boyfriends, so convincing you basically can't tell, but here, deactivated and stretched out on tables like in a morgue, they are disconcerting to look at, human but not quite human, not quite anything. You remember the name for this, uncanny valley, the way that they look like humans but are recognizably not humans.

Do you leave them deactivated like this all the time? you ask the older fat man, who has been watching you and smiling pleasantly for several minutes as you've wandered through the store.

When we get busy, I turn them all on, he says. Everything he says sounds very agreeable, like he was your uncle or father or grandfather speaking to you, as if he were enormously fond of you and you could tell that just from his voice. But on slow days like this, I let them rest, he says. Saves them some wear and tear.

I'm actually in the market for a new boyfriend, you say. You say this in a very conversational way, but what you really mean is, he should turn the boyfriends on because you are a paying customer. What you really mean is, the creepy morgue vibe of the boyfriend store is not making you want to purchase a boyfriend.

He looks you up and down, a quick swipe of his eyes. We're running a sale on floor models right now, he says, they've been lightly used here in the store, but we keep them in peak condition.

You realize that the older fat man thinks that you're poor, that you can't afford a brand new boyfriend. I have money, you say, and you realize that this is the clumsiest poor person thing you could have said.

What I mean is, you say, beginning again, I'm looking for something a little nicer.

Ah, well then, the older fat man says, Can I interest you in one of our custom models?

You feel that since you just said you had money, you can't turn around and ask the older fat man, who might actually be the CEO of the boyfriend manufacturer or possibly your uncle, how much a custom boyfriend would cost. You think of your savings. You have a lot of savings, you live frugally, you don't go on any expensive dates, you are good at your job and during the busy season, when your product is in demand, you earn a lot of bonuses and commissions on top of your salary. You're doing okay, so why not splurge a little bit? Still, the idea of spending some incredible amount of money, maybe five figures, makes you feel nervous, on edge. Maybe I am actually poor, you think.

The older fat man leads you to a computer near the back of the store. The screen shows a three-dimensional model of a boyfriend, and you can click on various parts and features to make the boyfriend what you want. You can click on his head and give him the kind of personality you want him to have, interests that would match yours, beliefs and values that you would have in common with him. There is even an option to tweak his voice so he sounds pleasing to you. The older fat man gestures at the machine and clearly you are supposed to use it to customize your boyfriend.

This level of god-like power makes you feel uncomfortable. You feel uncomfortable choosing your boyfriend's race, hair color, eye color. You feel uncomfortable assigning him a values system, religious beliefs. The boyfriends you've bought in the past have always been pleasing to you in their idiosyncrasies, the way that they are not ideal, the same way that a real boyfriend would not be ideal. The standard models are just like regular people, even after they learn to adjust to your particular needs, they are never quite perfect. You have never said, my boyfriend is perfect. You always imagined that if you had a real boyfriend, the flesh-and-blood kind, there would be things about him that would not necessarily be desirable. You have romantic notions about having a boyfriend, about opposites attracting, about loving someone that is imperfect.

Still, as you play around with the digital model of your potential boyfriend on the screen, the idea of a bespoke boyfriend appeals to you more and more. First, you give him blonde hair and green eyes and freckles, but also a tooth gap and a nose that looks like it's been broken. You change your mind about the freckles and give him a tan. You make his hair a little longer and then you make it a little blonder, so that it's almost white. You add a few inches of roots so that his hair looks like it has been dyed and is growing out. But after all that, and after adjusting his cheekbones and brow height and forehead length, you realize the overall effect is not terribly pleasing. He looks strange, alien, like he has maybe had too much plastic surgery or is trying too hard. You check the time and realize that you have already been customizing your boyfriend for hours. The older fat man looks at you knowingly, asks if you need any help in a tone that suggests that you might be in over your head. You don't need any help. Instead you hit the randomize button, and your boyfriend's features blur and change dramatically. You don't like that boyfriend either, so you reset to defaults and go back in to make the changes you want.

Freckles. You definitely wanted the freckles. The gap in his front teeth. The crooked smile. The nose that looks like it's been broken. It's been more hours, and that's just the face. You are an artist, you think. This is exactly what making art is like, you are pretty sure. This is also a little bit like what being God or a parent is like. You are making a human being. You make him look like an advertisement, like something out of a catalog. He is the exact generically handsome white man that would sell underwear in a Macy's catalog. Nothing about him is challenging to a white middle-class sensibility, which is the kind of sensibility that you have. You look at his beautiful, open face, and you think, there is nothing about him that would frighten or challenge me, and that's good. He might be unpredictable, but not too unpredictable.

After all that work on the face, the personality is a breeze, you want him to love attention, to enjoy the performing arts, to be funny, to be smart about the things you like. You make him bad at math. You make him very bad at math, almost cruelly bad at math. Of course you make him very neat. He loves to clean and do dishes because you hate cleaning and doing dishes. He likes long drives in the country followed by picnics on checkered blankets and skinny dipping in a warm pond. He likes wearing a suit and dancing very slow to very old music. He knows all the dances. There is a list of dances and you check mark every one of them.

You wave the older fat man over. I think this is the boyfriend I want, you say.

The older fat man goes over your options and makes small adjustments, gentle things, like changing out a favorite song, adding in a few memories of Europe, descriptions of class trips to the museum, a preference for tangerines. He tells you that he is correcting the common mistakes, things that everyone gets wrong. He smiles knowingly, like he knows what kind of boyfriend you want. He tells you that there is some extra memory space because you made your boyfriend so bad at math, so you decide that your boyfriend will also like comic books, just for the heck of it. Then you change your mind about the comic books, and instead give him some additional sex knowledge, some weird stuff that you don't even like. Maybe this will be the boyfriend you try weird sex stuff with. The older fat man tastefully averts his eyes.

The completed boyfriend costs fifteen thousand dollars, including the extended tech support package. You are so enamored of him you pay it, almost your entire savings, more than you ever thought you would spend on an artificial human being who would live with you and perform sexual favors and do some light housework. The older fat man smiles at you, tells you that it's worth it. It's still cheaper than a real husband, he says to you, and this is meant to sound friendly but for some reason it makes you feel bad, very bad, but just for a few seconds. You wonder if the older fat man has a husband or wife or perhaps a small group of polyamorous lovers that dote on him.

The boyfriend is delivered a week later. It took them some time to build him. He arrives in a long, white box that is almost exactly the dimensions of a coffin. You hurry the deliveryman inside so that the neighbors don't see him bringing a human-sized box into your house. Inside, your old boyfriend is dusting, arranging knick-knacks on a wood hutch, whistling a cheerful little song that came preprogrammed. You have listened to him whistle that cheerful little song for many years, and you begin to feel bad, deeply bad, like you did at the boyfriend store. Something in your torso between your heart and your stomach begins to ache.

Do you take away the old one? you ask the deliveryman, and he looks at you condescendingly and shakes his head, a tiny little shake that you take to mean that taking away your old boyfriend is absolutely not his job.

Call the company, the deliveryman says, they have a recycling program.

After the deliveryman leaves you stand in the living room with your hand on the soft matte surface of the white box for a long time while your boyfriend continues to whistle and dust in the background. You almost don't notice him, despite him being all that you are thinking about. You whistle along with his little tune. This is a very difficult time, you think. You've smudged the matte surface of the box with sweat from your hand. Surely the new boyfriend will get you through it.

You deactivate your old boyfriend gently, holding him in your arms as you press the power button. You kiss his cooling lips as his eyes go dark, and this reminds you of something you saw in a movie once. After, you hold his stiff body in your arms, his skin cold and rubbery. It is easier to think of him as something else, something it might be easy to someday send in to the boyfriend company's recycling program. But for now, you can't quite bear the thought. Instead, you prop him up in your hall closet, next to the vacuum cleaner and a box of Christmas decorations that didn't make it up to the attic and some winter coats, size medium, that don't fit you anymore.

With your old boyfriend safely stored, you begin to feel more comfortable opening up the new boyfriend. The top

ZACHARY DOSS ❦ 65

of the box slides off easily, despite its size, and inside the new boyfriend is carefully packaged for travel, nestled in a Styrofoam groove carved to exactly his dimensions. Otherwise he is naked. You touch his skin, running your finger along his neck and chest, and even turned off his skin feels more real than your old boyfriend's, so real that you can't believe you ever thought your old boyfriend was exactly the same as a real person.

You power him on, and he is already fully charged. He has the new power cell, invented by the boyfriend company, and his charge will last for days, maybe a week if he's not doing much. It is a very good power cell, you read a lot of articles on it when it was first invented. Charges instantly, lasts forever was the copy they used for the headline, an exaggeration, obviously, but still, you were very excited about the possibility of not having to charge your boyfriend every 12 hours to make sure he didn't shut off unexpectedly.

The new boyfriend sits up and stretches, arching his back and sighing. He scratches his balls and looks around. I like your house, he says.

You aren't sure what algorithm he has used to decide that your house is to his taste. Unlike your old boyfriend, whose processing was very easy to detect and follow, the new boyfriend has a kind of casualness, as if speaking off the cuff, as if these are his actual opinions. You look around to try to see what he sees, but however he has determined that he likes your house, it isn't obvious to you. Probably he just did a quick search of decorating and architecture blogs, you think, but you are also a little mystified by your boyfriend having an opinion like that, volunteered unprompted.

The new boyfriend mostly walks around naked for the first few days. You feel uncomfortable giving him access to your old boyfriend's clothes, which you still somewhat superstitiously consider his belongings. You know that the old boyfriend, and the new boyfriend, for that matter, are not actually people, but technology that you have purchased, same as your ice machine or your television or your treadmill. But you can't quite get away from the imagined narrative that you and your old boyfriend have broken up, and you subsequently replaced him with someone younger and hotter. You have been socialized to believe that this is wrong. You are pretty sure that you would consider that a dick move if someone else did it to a real person, but you remind yourself that your old boyfriend was not a real person. Just in case, you avoid the hall closet.

You and the new boyfriend get used to each other. It is a slow process. He doesn't whistle, but he plays music while he does his housework. He sings along with the songs you selected for him to like. He dances, shakes his hips and bobs his head. When you ask about the dancing, he tells you how he went to school for dance, studied for a time in France, got his MFA. You don't remember programming any of this in. You made vague selections, but you guess that if someone likes being the center of attention, loves music, loves the performing arts, dance would actually be a good occupation. You remember that you wanted him to know how to do all of the dances.

He's not uncomfortable being naked. You bring up the subject of clothes and he shrugs at you. I'd like to have something nice to wear if we go out, he says.

What kinds of clothes do you like? you ask him.

The kinds of clothes that the new boyfriend likes are very expensive. You want him to be happy, so you get him a few things to wear, but having depleted your savings, you are now dipping into your paycheck, meaning that instead of putting more money into savings, you are spending it all on the new boyfriend. You become very worried about money, you are poorer than you have ever been. Thinking of the avuncular man at the boyfriend store, you don't talk about your financial woes with the new boyfriend.

Still, some of the clothing you purchase for the new boyfriend is more for your benefit than his. You give him some sexy underwear, fancy stuff, and clothes that it wouldn't be appropriate for him to wear out. You expect him to wear the sexy stuff around the house but most days he wears baggy sweatpants and a tank top. You never bought him baggy sweatpants or a tank top, so you're not sure where he got them. Like most things about him, this is very mysterious to you. He is a real surprise, an actual surprise, you're never quite sure what he's going to do. You discover that he knows how to shop online, has been using your credit card without your permission. You are now in debt, granted a very small amount of debt, but debt just the same.

You are as angry at him as you would be if he were a real boyfriend. You are fascinated as well as angry, because you have never felt this before, anger at the person you are in a relationship with, but that doesn't stop you from yelling, demanding that he ask your permission before going off and spending money like that. He is angry too, you can tell he's angry because of the way his whole face darkens, the way the change descends on him in a sudden rush. All of a sudden you are in your first fight. A screaming match. You try to turn the volume on your boyfriend down, but the newest model doesn't come with a volume adjustment and instead you stand very still while he yells at you.

You expect this to be the last of your problems, but they continue. It is still the slow season at work, an unusually long slow season, and you're concerned about money. You stay home all weekend, sitting in the dark to preserve power, eating cheap food out of a can. Your new boyfriend asks if you can go out, have a picnic, or maybe see some theater, but you refuse, you can't afford the gas to drive out to the country, and theater tickets are certainly out of the question.

Your boyfriend stops singing and dancing as he does his housework. He frowns a lot. He moves slowly through his chores, cleaning and dusting and doing dishes in a way that you might describe as resentful. He seems to be sulking. You try to make it up to him, pay extra attention, compliment him on his clothes, his hair, his taste in movies. Secretly, you consult the manual, but you find nothing there, or in the online message boards, that explains what's wrong with your boyfriend. So few people have bought the custom model (the deluxe custom model, you discover, is in fact what you've purchased) that there are hardly any posts at all. Finally, you call customer support. You have a short conversation with a man who you swear is the same man that sold you your boyfriend, the same happy uncle voice, and he remotely accesses your boyfriend's hard drive and tells you that your boyfriend is functioning perfectly. You persist, try to explain that there's something wrong, but the customer support person hangs up on you.

At night, your boyfriend asks you to try the strange sex things that you programmed him to like. You still don't like any of those things, start to go through the motions and then stop, make another jerky, awkward effort, but you find you just can't do it. He looks at you impatiently, makes disappointed noises. He doesn't say that he's having a bad time, but it's clear from his body language that you are not meeting his expectations. When you pause, again, in the middle of attempting the weird sex, he scoffs in frustration and leaves. You're alone in bed with the mess, disappointed and horny. Maybe you like the weird sex thing after all, you just don't want to actually do it or have it done to you. Your boyfriend sleeps on the couch.

After all that, you can't sleep. You stay awake, staring at the ceiling, feeling confused and sad and furious. The new boyfriend has not been at all what you expected, which is something very much like the old boyfriend but better. The new boyfriend is more realistic but you realize that this isn't better. This isn't what you wanted. You stumble downstairs, to the hall closet, where you push the too-small coats aside and look at the old boyfriend, who appears to be sleeping. You touch his face and it's so cold. You can't bring yourself to activate him, look him in the face, explain why he's been sitting in the hall closet for weeks. Instead you shut the door and wander down to the living room, where the new boyfriend is sleeping on the couch. You roughly shake him awake. You don't need to sleep anyway, you say angrily.

I appreciate the time to myself, he says, and he even sounds appropriately groggy.

I want to fuck you, you say. Even you can hear how angry you sound.

Do what you want, he says. You do what you want. Afterward, he says nothing, just shrugs and curls back up on the couch, wraps the blanket even more tightly around himself. You wander upstairs, passing the hall closet, checking it twice to make sure it's closed.

Over a period of days the new boyfriend continues to function more and more poorly. He refuses to do his chores. He burns his clothes, and then orders new clothes. He burns your clothes, and doesn't buy new ones. Also, there's the crying, he cries nonstop, sitting on the bed or the couch or at the kitchen table with his head in his hands. They are deep, convincing sobs, he sounds like a real person crying, and the part of you that instinctively reacts to a fellow human's sadness feels profoundly upset at the way that your boyfriend is crying. You have to remind yourself several times a day that he is not real, not a real person.

You try to call the company again, talk to the man who is like your uncle, so kind, to see if he will maybe take the boyfriend back, the boyfriend who you are convinced is defective. You have a long conversation with the man on the phone where you somehow do not return the boyfriend. Again, the man is convinced that there is nothing wrong with your boyfriend, that he is behaving in exactly the correct way. That's impossible, you say. All he does is cry. But the man at the boyfriend company is unhelpful. The return policy is more unhelpful.

You attempt to sell the boyfriend, put an ad on the internet and in the newspaper, but nobody wants him. You are honest in the ad, say that the boyfriend has not stopped crying in weeks, no longer does or says anything to you. I think it might just be me, you write. You might have better luck. Nobody answers your ad, nor does anyone respond to your post on the message board asking for advice or possibly technical information that might allow you to reprogram your boyfriend.

Finally, you come home one day and the new boyfriend has pulled the old boyfriend out of the hall closet. You wonder how the new boyfriend came to discover the old boyfriend. The old boyfriend is spread out on the floor, arms spread like a cross, and the new boyfriend is cutting the old boyfriend with a kitchen knife, your good chef's knife. He is digging into the old boyfriend's torso with the knife, reaching in and pulling out handfuls of wiring. Is this what I look like on the inside? he asks.

I guess so, you say, maybe newer or nicer. I don't really know. You are buried in sadness, mourning, you realize, because your old boyfriend is now gone forever and never coming back. You can't even be angry at the new boyfriend, you are just numb, in shock.

Is this what you're going to do with me? Replace me with something else? he asks. You swear that his hand, still holding the knife, is trembling.

Probably not, you say, you were very expensive. And anyway, I've just realized that I loved that boyfriend. I'm sad that you killed him.

I hate you, the new boyfriend says.

The new boyfriend screams and hacks the old boyfriend's head off with the kitchen knife. You keep your distance, wondering if you can reach for your phone without him noticing. The new boyfriend seems inconsolable, screaming and hacking and now crying again, crying more. I think you're malfunctioning, you say, trying to be very calm.

YOU'RE malfunctioning, he screams, and lunges at you with the knife.

You see him moving at you too late, his arm swinging the knife toward your throat at slightly faster-than-human speed. Your hand is wrapped around your cell phone, but you're already too slow, you realize it's too late. Still, the thing you feel saddest about is the old boyfriend, spread out on the floor, his torso shredded, his head hanging from his neck by his spine, which you see is made of what looks like a high-density ceramic. The knife chipped it but didn't break. He looks so broken, a dead thing, and that space between your heart and your stomach tightens and twists inside you.

Maybe I am malfunctioning, you think, and nothing more after that.

IV

You Love it All so Goddamn Much

Esquire

IT IS SOMETHING that you notice very suddenly. You are standing in the checkout line holding a sack of limes and you realize that the cashier is your boyfriend. He wears a wig that is long and chestnut-colored and has a slight wave to it. This hair is nothing like your boyfriend's hair. It could be your imagination, but it seems your boyfriend, wearing a bald cap, is also bagging your groceries, making a face at your unripe bananas.

It's possible that you are just having a bad afternoon, except all week you don't run into anyone who isn't your boyfriend. Your boyfriend in dreadlocks hands you your cup of coffee. Your boyfriend in an undershirt jogs through the park while your boyfriend in an extremely fancy car cuts you off in traffic. You go to the gym and your boyfriend sits at the front desk when you check in, your boyfriend hands you a towel, your boyfriend has already worked up a sweat by the time you make it to the weight room. You are at a club late one night and you have unprotected sex in the bathroom with your boyfriend, who is on his break from dancing on a glowing platform.

You go to your therapist, who is also your boyfriend, and you feel uncomfortable telling him about your feelings.

Let's say I am your boyfriend, your boyfriend says, being your therapist, with glasses and unflattering lipstick. What is it you feel like you couldn't tell me?

In your hands, you hold a magazine that you carried with you from the waiting room. You couldn't put it down. You twist it nervously, bending the pages into a semi-permanent tube. Your boyfriend is on the cover, wearing a well-tailored suit and grinning and suddenly you can feel him looking at you from every direction. You look over at a lamp and it is your boyfriend, and the computer, your boyfriend, your therapist's chair is your boyfriend and the chair you are sitting on is your boyfriend and the bookcase is your boyfriend and the desk and the diploma on the wall is your boyfriend the whole room is your boyfriend and the sky outside the trees the cars the roads the buildings the earth, everything is your boyfriend and you love it, you love it all so goddamn much.

Sex Stuff

YOUR BOYFRIEND WORKS in pornography. You thought this might bother you but it doesn't bother you at all. Your boyfriend travels to Florida or California or Texas for work. You notice pornography is filmed where it is hot outside and the sun is always shining. Your boyfriend is never called to Maine or Minnesota or Wisconsin to film pornography. Which is fine, you are unconcerned that the weather other places might be better. Your boyfriend deposits his pornography paychecks in your joint bank account, and it doesn't bother you to see his income listed on your bank statements. You make about the same amount of money, which is cool. That is totally cool with you, that your boyfriend is doing enough pornography to make a regular income. Your best friend calls you up to tell you he saw your boyfriend on the internet doing some sex stuff. It doesn't bother you that he says it like that, sex stuff. You're proud of what your boyfriend does for a living. You are proud of your boyfriend and, most importantly, you are not bothered that your best friend called you up. You and your boyfriend have sex sometimes. While you are having sex you imagine your boyfriend having sex with other people and it doesn't bother you that imagining your boyfriend having sex with other people is more arousing than imagining your boyfriend having sex with you. After, you lay in bed next to your boyfriend and it doesn't bother you that you don't have muscle definition or visible abs. You are awake, your eyes open, long after your boyfriend has fallen asleep. It's getting hotter outside, global warming, probably, and that doesn't bother you, you are not bothered at all.

Fraternal

YOUR BOYFRIEND HAS a twin brother. They look nothing alike but your boyfriend is always trying to play tricks on you as if he and his brother are identical. Often your boyfriend's twin brother shows up on dates you planned with your boyfriend, giggling because he has played a trick on you.

Going on a date with your boyfriend's twin brother, who takes great pains to talk and act like your boyfriend, is almost the same as going on a date with your boyfriend, even though your boyfriend's twin brother looks nothing like your boyfriend and has a terrible personality. He eats the things your boyfriend likes, gives a reasonable imitation of your boyfriend's opinions. At the end of each night, your boyfriend jumps out of the bushes and shouts, I caught you! Out on a date with my twin brother. Sometimes this happens in public and people laugh and clap because they think you are doing a play.

Your boyfriend and his twin brother try to do other twin things. They talk in a secret language you don't understand, only actually they're speaking Spanish and you understand everything. They try to solve mysteries. They wear the same clothes or radically different clothes. We switched places once, to try to trick our parents into getting back together, your boyfriend tells you.

But it could be your boyfriend's twin brother who tells you this. You are on a date, and you can't tell if your boyfriend and his brother have switched places or not. You find that you can no longer tell them apart. This might be your boyfriend's twin brother, or maybe your boyfriend is having a bad day. This might be your boyfriend, or maybe your boyfriend's twin brother got an unflattering haircut. In your mind, their features have begun to blur together. You decide to be in a relationship with whichever one you are nearest at the time.

It didn't work, your boyfriend says. It was very disappointing.

The Problem-Solver

WITH YOUR BOYFRIEND, something urgent is always happening. Maybe he's in a fight with his best friend, or someone at his job got murdered and he's got a lead on the killer, or he has a project due at 8 a.m. and he's overslept, or he's pretty sure someone is following him everywhere he goes, but he can't talk about it. Some days you only see your boyfriend at meals, but he never gets to eat, much less have a conversation. He gets a call when the fork is halfway to his mouth. He gets a text just as he's folding his slice of pizza in half. He cuts a neat triangle from his waffle and just then, someone bursts through the door with news.

When your boyfriend calls out for delivery, he asks for two cheeseburgers, extra fries, a side of the special chili, macaroni and cheese with extra cheese, fried pickles. At breakfast he asks for waffles, sausage, biscuits and gravy, a spinach and feta omelet, extra bacon, breakfast tacos, mini blueberry muffins. He always orders two pizzas instead of one, extra breadsticks with his lasagna, he always tells the waiter he wants an appetizer. He orders all this food and then he can't eat it because he is called away. He is running toward something or he is running away from something. He is dropping his fork to rush out the door; he is dropping a full cup of frozen yogurt to melt as he runs down the street.

Your boyfriend's hunger is magnified, legendary. He can't eat even when he tries. When he lifts a fork to his mouth, even an empty fork, an alarm goes off somewhere in the distance. He knows he's the only one who can solve these problems, from the minor crisis to the major catastrophe. He has to be there to stop the nuclear plant from melting down. He has to be there to save his best friend's marriage. In his wake he leaves a trail of solved problems, satisfied customers, citizens saved, and a trail of rot, a landfill's worth of food waste, never eaten, the hollow inside him growing at an incredible rate even as he sometimes looks over his shoulder with longing.

Once, he ignored a crisis, tried to take a bite despite the alarm going off in the distance, and a second alarm went off, then more, a falling building in midtown, a tidal wave at the beach, a plane falling out of the sky, a civil war erupting across Europe, an entire landmass cracking off and falling into the sea, and as his tongue touched just the smallest bit of his ravioli, the sun went supernova, dooming the world billions of years from now, when the wave of fire finally reaches Earth.

He could never bring himself to do it again.

It is hard to say to him, you are always leaving me, but he is always leaving you, surrounded by piles of uneaten food, discarded, another thing he wants but dares not touch his mouth to. You are lonely among the worms and ants that emerge from hiding to pick at scraps of egg, the rare beetles hoping to steal a pepperoni, the birds flying away with dinner rolls and the rats nibbling at discarded cheeseburgers. Here is what your boyfriend does not do: come back. Here is what you do not do: chase after him. Even though he leaves a trail you could easily follow, you are not a scavenger, and you don't need anything from him.

Higher Learning

YOUR BOYFRIEND ENROLLS in community college without discussing it with you, which is the kind of thing he's always doing. I thought some fresh air would do me good, your boyfriend says.

You aren't pleased, but you want your boyfriend to have a good experience at community college, so you go with him to the store to get a nice tent, a sleeping bag that's warm enough, a gas lamp. You and your boyfriend spend some time standing together silently looking at fishing poles. Do you know how to fish? you ask your boyfriend.

Community college is about learning, you know? he says. Maybe in community college I'll learn things about fishing. You get him a fishing pole just in case.

When you drop your boyfriend off at community college, you are surprised to discover that you feel nervous for him. You want him to succeed and be liked. You want him to get good grades and improve his life. As he walks to the cabins, you notice that he seems much older than everyone else at community college. You feel one last stab of hope that he'll fit in. You don't know if he packed enough clean underwear.

It takes about a week of you sitting at home alone, drinking wine and feeling apprehensive, for the first letter from your boyfriend to arrive from community college. The letter sets you at ease. Your boyfriend is doing the usual community college things, making arts and crafts, singing around the campfire, learning to swim, participating in a late-night panty raid on the girls' community college on the other side of the lake. He tells you, his excitement present in the letter, that he has learned to make his own lip balm. He doesn't mention if he's used the fishing pole.

You remember your time at community college. It was very different. The sky was always dark, incipient rain never falling, the clouds heavy. There was a problem with ghosts in the cabins and lake monsters in the lake, and the slashed bodies of the other students were always turning up in bushes and under picnic tables or washing up on the beach. Your boyfriend says nothing about lake monsters in his letter, although he does say that sometimes he hears other students crying in their bunks, homesick. Nobody was homesick when you went to community college, but then, you went to a better community college than your boyfriend.

When the last day of community college comes and you can finally go pick your boyfriend up, it is a beautiful day, the sun shining over the lake and the picnic tables and the long wood cabins. There is enough time for you to walk with your boyfriend around the lake, where he points out all the places that he had fun while he was at community college. He shows you the cabin he stayed in, and the bunk, his name written on a chalkboard hung at the foot of his bed with twine, the spot at the lake where he did finally use the fishing pole, the sandy rectangle where they played volleyball. He introduces you to his community college teachers, who say kind things, are generally pleased with his abilities, the way that he can macramé a lanyard, how well he does at making his own all-natural beeswax lip balm, how attractive the birdhouses he made were to the local birds.

They all hug him, one by one, and thank him for being such a good student at community college. They shake your hand. In the parking lot, the other students are filing out to where parents and loved ones are eager to take them home. It's a chaotic scene, lots of shouting, a churning crowd. Your boyfriend runs off to say his goodbyes to his fellow students. You grin and pop the trunk of your car, where you have a ski mask, and an axe, and a real educational experience.

V

*You Did the Things
That Made Sense to You*

You Could Fucking Sell That

YOUR BOYFRIEND RUNS for president as an outsider political candidate. You try not to let this disturb your life too much although your boyfriend is always on the television and the radio and satellite radio and the internet. He gives interviews in the home you share and you aren't there for any of them, you don't even try to be. His slogan is Turn it around, America! and your slogan is This is none of my business. You have a very important business that is actually your business and you make the money your boyfriend uses to run for president as an outsider political candidate and otherwise you want nothing to do with it.

Eventually you agree to one interview. Short, very short, I'm very busy, you say a little sharply to your boyfriend's campaign manager, who called you at the office. You agree mostly to get him off the phone.

Never call me at the office, you text your boyfriend, even though he's not even the one who called you.

You sit down for the interview with a woman who has a very broad, sensitive face. Before the cameras start rolling, you watch her do facial exercises to stretch out her face muscles. At first, she looks gently concerned and you're about to ask her what her problem is, but then she laughs too loudly and then she frowns deeply and then, excruciatingly, begins to fake cry, which she is not good at. Then she makes a series of very loud noises, stretching her face to its extremes one way or the other, before finally setting into her default facial expression, a very placid affair you described initially as sensitive. She wears spring colors, pastel pinks and yellows, and you wonder whether it's spring. You have no idea if it's spring or not, but her eyeshadow matches her outfit and her eyes, closed while she practices her weep-moaning, remind you of Easter eggs.

She smiles and begins your interview.

Later, you are on all of the shows. People describe you as unlikeable. They talk about how you were too sharp or too mean or too smart or your suit was too grey. Almost charcoal, a very large potato-looking man snarls on his talk show. You wore a grey suit and a black shirt, you smiled but it seemed insincere, you run a very profitable business and are worth billions of dollars and you are not good for the environment or minorities or the economy. Your hair was expertly, beautifully styled. You looked sexy but unapproachable. The American people hate you.

The American people hate you, your boyfriend's campaign manager says over the phone. He clears his throat several times as he talks. You wonder if he hates you too. You wonder if he and your boyfriend have become lovers on the campaign trail. You wonder if your company has a film and television division, because you could sell that story. You could fucking sell that.

You are about to respond that you hate the American people too, but your boyfriend's campaign manager hangs up on you. Almost immediately your face on the TV screen is replaced by your boyfriend standing in a half embrace with the Trash Pope, both men waving with their free hands. The Trash Pope looks benevolent, which you suppose is basically his full-time job anyway. The pundits describe this as a coup for your boyfriend, leading to sharp polling increases among Americans who practice the Trash Religion. When the TV show cuts away from your boyfriend and the Trash Pope, all that remains is a ticker across the bottom of the screen that reads, Popular political candidate has awful boyfriend, has secured the endorsement of the Trash Pope.

You sense a but belongs in that sentence somewhere. Instead, it seems like the two things are connected. Your boyfriend finally responds to your text, with a brief email asking for more money and referring to you as his campaign's largest donor.

On election night, you stand on the stage with your boyfriend and his campaign manager and dozens of people you don't recognize, people you assume worked on your boyfriend's campaign. You're pretty sure one of the men is a high-ranking official in the Trash Church. Your boyfriend has a strong lead in the exit polls and everyone is smiling at each other. There is an outrageous amount of smiling. The campaign manager suggests you and your boyfriend engage in some celebratory affection, a hug or a kiss or a head-butt. You ignore him and he head-butts your boyfriend instead.

The assassination seems to come from nowhere. The sniper rifle makes a loud crack, still barely audible above the noise of the crowd. Your boyfriend is one state away from winning the electoral college. It's Florida, you think, maybe it's Florida. You catch your boyfriend as he falls back. It's a high-caliber bullet, the kind that leaves both an entrance hole and an exit hole.

As you sit, cradling your boyfriend's mostly exploded head, you think of the first lady who, under similar circumstances, tried to keep her husband's brains contained within his head long enough for help to arrive. You think of the First Lady who, shortly after her husband was killed, went mad. You desperately wish you were that kind of lover, but you don't feel ready to do either of those things. While you are kneeling in front of maybe twenty thousand people with your dead boyfriend's brains all over your charcoal-colored suit, your face is carefully blank.

Your boyfriend wins Florida and the election, and the campaign manager is sobbing, and you think, yeah, you could definitely fucking sell that.

Spatial Awareness

YOU AND YOUR boyfriend move into one of those houses that are so small everything has to be more than one thing. The only piece of furniture is modular. Your couch folds out into a bed, and then folds a different way into a bookcase, and then folds a different way into an exercise machine. The house is only one room, except for the closet, which has all your clothes hanging in it, and below that, a toilet. If you take all the clothes out of the closet and remove the bar that they hang on, there is a showerhead, so you can shower awkwardly half-kneeling on the toilet seat.

To move into the small house, you and your boyfriend had to get rid of many of your possessions. You bagged everything up, planning to donate to Goodwill, but your boyfriend said you were thinking about your possessions in the wrong way. He unbagged everything you had carefully decided to donate and put it back where it belonged. He gave you one medium-sized box. Put everything you want to take with you in this box. After you filled the box, which held less than half of what you really wanted to take with you, your boyfriend helped you load it into your car. Then, he locked the door to your large house, splashed a little gasoline on the outside, and lit it on fire.

Being minimal requires commitment, your boyfriend said.

You made a list of the things in the house you would have liked to sneak off with, things that didn't make it into the small box. The heat of your burning house bathed the front lawn in a kind of desert heat. You remembered to get the dog out, right? you asked.

In the small house, even the dog is pulling double duty. You can't keep more than one pet in the small house, so the dog has to be more than one pet. You decide that, from the right angle, the dog looks a lot like a cat, a bigger, hairier breed of cat, like maybe a Maine Coon. You name the dog Julia, and the cat Suzanne. When the dog chases its own tail, you imagine that the dog is chasing the cat.

It is immediately apparent that your boyfriend is not prepared for your cramped life in the small house. He is used to reading on the couch while you nap in your bed, but because the bed is also the couch, you can't do both at the same time. When he wants to get a book, he has to wait for you to finish your set of bench presses. The few possessions you kept fit awkwardly into the house. Everything is visible all the time. To your boyfriend, it looks like clutter. One day, when you come home, you find your small box of possessions sitting on the curb with your trashcan. The trashcan is almost as big as the house, you think. From outside, you can see your boyfriend through the windows. He is trying to make dinner and trips because he left the wrong drawer open.

Later, all the drawers are empty and taped shut. Together you and your boyfriend share one pan, one bowl, and one spoon. One person eats first, and then washes the dishes, and then the next person eats. Your boyfriend always eats first, which you think is unfair, so you make a color-coded calendar with an eating schedule and a dishwashing schedule and even a weightlifting and reading and napping schedule. After one day, the calendar disappears, and you never see it again. Your boyfriend tells you that the dog ate it, but you haven't seen the dog in a few days either. Your boyfriend tells you that the dog ran away.

I wish I could run away, you say.

Don't be shitty, your boyfriend says.

Without the dog or any possessions, there seems to be more room in the tiny house. But you and your boyfriend still get in each other's way, bonk heads or crack shins. You decide that this is just a natural part of adjusting to life in the tiny house, but your boyfriend is temperamental, furious. He is determined to make this work. He keeps saying that, I am determined to make this work. He stops sleeping as much, sitting awake next to you, and when the sun rises, he has dark hollows around his eyes.

Soon, you get sick. You can't seem to keep food down, instead throwing up all day. You throw up at your job while people look nervous. Eventually your boss sends you home because you are throwing up every hour and your coworkers are uncomfortable. When you get home, you head straight to the tiny bathroom. You have diarrhea all afternoon. You sit on the toilet with your head smothered between two of your suit coats. One of them is slightly damp, you discover, because the showerhead leaks.

This illness lasts for some time. You get sicker and sicker. You get very thin. You take up very little space in the tiny house. Most of the time you sit on the toilet, in the closet. Occasionally you go out and drink water and eat some of the food your boyfriend has prepared for you, soup and crackers and big bottles of red Gatorade. The red Gatorade makes it look like you are vomiting blood. The toilet closet starts to smell bad, and then the entire small house starts to smell bad. You lose your job, but that's okay, because you'll probably die very soon.

You're glad you moved to the small house; it is very economical and your boyfriend can afford to live there by himself.

Washington, Adams, Jefferson, Madison

IT IS THE end of the world for both of you. In the spare room you don't talk about with each other anymore, your boyfriend sits with a pile of flashcards, flipping them over, one after another. He doesn't say anything by way of identifying what is on the card. It's a motion, a pattern. Flip, recognize, flip again. Each card features a cheerful caricature of a former President of the United States set on a yellow background. Earlier he took the living presidents out, set them on the window ledge to bleach in the sun. Jimmy Carter, Bill Clinton, the George Bushes, Senior and Junior. Barack Obama.

You try to be with him for several hours every day. At first, you sing the Presidents Song in your head. Washington, Adams, Jefferson, Madison, Monroe, Adams, Jackson, while he silently flips cards. The song is a device you remember from your elementary school class. Somehow, they thought it was important, knowing the names of all the presidents. That was a long time ago; now, you never get any further than Jackson, humming the rest of the song without remembering the words. You watch your boyfriend carefully, waiting for his lips to move, but they don't.

He doesn't even look at the cards, although he pauses on each one for long enough to see, if he were looking.

Otherwise you maintain your normal routine. You go to work early in the morning so you can come home a little earlier in the afternoon. Your job has been very accommodating. The Monday after, your boss tells you to take all the time you need, and you tell him that it will feel good just to have something else to focus on. This, too, felt rehearsed. You don't know if it feels better to be at work or not. You don't want to leave your boyfriend alone, but you know he is alone whether you are there or not. At work you feel alone, but also like a robot, or something automatic. You go through the motions. You laugh at jokes. Nobody notices that you have taken down all of the pictures that sat on your desk.

The night you came home from the hospital the house seemed impossibly warm. You checked the thermostat, and, sure enough, it was over eighty degrees. The air conditioner was broken. You fussed with the thermostat and then went out to the back yard to look at the AC unit. Your boyfriend was almost crying, shook his head and said, leave it, just leave it and his voice trembled. You stood outside on the dry grass in your bare feet and examined the AC unit with your flashlight. It wasn't running, you couldn't hear any noise, the fan wasn't spinning. Nothing. You didn't know what it was supposed to look like, but not like this. Something's wrong with it, you said out loud.

You thought your boyfriend was on the porch, but he had already gone inside. You went room to room, opened all the windows, but really you were looking for him. You found him in the spare room, and you almost didn't open the door, but then you did. Your boyfriend was sitting on the tiny bed, his weight wrinkling the comforter, which was covered in cheerful trains. There had been an argument about the cheerful trains; your boyfriend thought they were too gendered, but you held out for them. He was holding, in one hand, the kind of brightly-colored, soft, noisy toy that a baby could play with and chew on and throw at the cat. Around the lump forming in your throat, right at the bottom of your skull, you remembered joking that it looked like some kind of sex toy. In his other hand, he had the Presidents of the United States flashcards. The package is branded SmartBaby™ and has a cartoon baby wearing a mortarboard and holding a diploma.

He would have been such a smart baby, you think, and the weight of the night sits on you. When your sister agreed to carry the baby for you and your boyfriend, nobody thought much of it at all. It seemed like the easiest thing in the world. She was one of those women who loved being pregnant. She had three already and her husband didn't want a fourth, and then you asked her if she would mind. Sure, she said. One more for the road.

Your sister made it, but just barely. The baby didn't. That night, neither you nor your boyfriend slept. You did the things that made the most sense to you, made a pot of tea, cleaned the kitchen, called your mother to let her know your sister was doing fine. You heard your boyfriend crying, although you knew realistically you couldn't hear him from across the house, over the sound of running water. You forced yourself still, told yourself you needed to finish the dishes. It was a little before sunrise and your neighbors were starting to wake up.

When you finished the dishes, you went back to the spare room to find your boyfriend wrapped in the train blanket, turning over the flashcards. His eyes were dry, and he was staring absently at the mural you'd had custom-painted on the bedroom wall. Later, you will want to paint over the mural, but your boyfriend won't. You asked him if he wanted to come to bed, but he just looked at you and kept turning over cards. Washington. Adams. Jefferson. Madison. James Madison, the fourth President of the United States, smiled a happy cartoon smile up from the flash card. Neither of you could stop looking at him. When you heard the sound of your neighbor's car starting, the beginning of his morning commute, you started crying, and then you were both crying. It was supposed to be his room, and then it wasn't.

The Purses

YOUR BOYFRIEND HAS a room full of handbags, which you are not allowed to enter. You have always been particularly annoyed about the room full of handbags because after all there's a whole room in your apartment you're apparently not allowed to use because it's full of handbags. This is how you phrase it when you argue with him about it, there's a whole room in my apartment I'm apparently not allowed to use because it's full of handbags.

You try to explain to your boyfriend the other uses you might put that room to, and really, you can imagine all sorts of things. We could have a private exercise room, you say over dinner. We could have an office, you say as you walk your dog around the park. We could fill it with fish tanks and have a fish tank room, you whisper into his ear at a friend's cocktail party. It goes on like this, with you proposing alternate uses for the room: library, greenhouse, spare bedroom, yoga studio, second kitchen, second living room, racquetball court, art gallery, movie theater, indoor swimming pool, sauna.

Your boyfriend is always carrying a handbag hooked in his elbow, a clutch held at his side, or a tiny backpack over his shoulder. Your boyfriend has the most fashionable handbags. He has the expensive kind and the really expensive kind, a gleaming crocodile leather Birkin, a pristine white Chanel that you are pretty sure has actual diamonds in the clasp, an ugly limited edition Louis Vuitton designed by some woman you have never heard of. He has the less expensive kinds, too, the kind your mom used to buy at Macy's, the Michael Kors and the Dooney & Burke and the Coach. The regular bags he carries every day to work and parties and the gym. The expensive bags you rarely see, although he often spends hours alone with them in his handbag room.

You have always wondered what the inside of the handbag room looks like. You are not interested in the handbags but you burn to walk inside that secret room and witness the alchemy of them all arrayed together like hieroglyphs. You dream that it is beautiful, each purse a jewel, carefully placed on labeled glass shelves. The light from the window floods the room and refracts through the glass shelves, each handbag reclining in its warm little sunspot like a cat. In your dream you weep because the handbag room is actually heaven. In your dream you open the diamond-encrusted clasp of the white Chanel and you crawl inside, curl up, and rub your cheek against the pink silk lining. The clasp closes behind you but the lining seems to glow with light from the outside. Inside the white Chanel purse is a smaller purse covered in black feathers, its provenance unknown to you. In the pink darkness, you wait for your boyfriend to find you, clutching the smaller black purse to your chest and gently stroking its silky feathers.

Despite your persistence, your boyfriend seems uninterested in the non-handbag potential of his handbag room.

When you say, finally, that it might be nice to have an extra room for a nursery, just in case, he rolls his eyes at you before taking another gulp from his glass of wine. He doesn't say anything more, but you understand the discussion regarding the room full of handbags is officially closed.

Transubstantiation

YOU AND YOUR boyfriend sit on the porch and watch the sun set. To call it a porch is really a kind of elevation or even glorification. Really, you set two chairs and a table and a pot of flowers on the sidewalk outside your apartment door and called it your porch. You are always worried someone passing by will smash your flower pot. That's just the kind of person you are. You are sharing a cigarette with your boyfriend, passing it back and forth. Whenever you hand the cigarette off to him, your fingers touch briefly. You have no language for the kind of intimacy you feel, like you are the same person smoking one cigarette, only not.

The view from your porch, which is not really a porch, is devastatingly bad. Spread out in front of you is a parking lot and across the parking lot is an apartment building that looks just like your apartment building, and both buildings are unremarkable but ugly. They are squat and painted brown, brown everywhere, 3 or 4 different shades of muddy brown. To see the sun set you have to look up and over the top of the other building. Behind that building there are some trees, and a much prettier apartment complex, and you watch the sun turn orange and then so red and heavy it bruises the sky purple. You pretend that you don't feel the heat coming off the asphalt and you don't see all the cars parked in rows or the mud-colored apartment building across the parking lot. You pretend that the prettier building, the one with the trees, is where you and your boyfriend live.

Really, you are thinking about killing yourself. It is a passive and familiar feeling. You often feel this way. You thought having a boyfriend would make you want to live, but you still hate yourself, and you do not hate yourself less because he loves you; instead this has simply increased the sensation you have that you are a disappointment, to him and to everyone. You are the kind of person who imagines running his car into the freeway median at seventy miles an hour, but you aren't sure yet whether you'd actually do it. Everything you feel is so sleepy and passive, a painfully bearable kind of numbness. You feel guilty for thinking about killing yourself when your boyfriend loves you, like you are too selfish to love him more than you hate yourself. You're that kind of person.

Your boyfriend is thinking about how his parents were once very rich but now they are very poor. That's the kind of life he's had, like when your foot slips off a rung on a ladder and you're on your back on the ground before you know it. A head-cracked-in kind of life. A thirty-stitches kind of life. At least, that's the way he thinks about it, until your fingers brush his again, and then he thinks about your beautiful long fingers that are going yellowish-brown at the first knuckle, where the cigarette rests, even though it seems like you are both too young for that kind of discoloration. Your boyfriend hasn't had that hard of a life, really, but just possesses the kind of naiveté that leads young people to think that their difficult experiences are the most difficult possible experiences. He's that kind of person.

When the sky fades and goes dark, your boyfriend takes the last drag of your last cigarette of the evening, and instead of lighting a new one from its burning tip, he grinds the living ember out on the sole of his shoe, right beneath the ball of his foot. When he leans over to do this, you watch him, and you think for a moment you see him from an angle you've never seen before, and he becomes something else. Because you're watching him, you become something else too, and that feeling ripples out until everything, the pavement and the cars, the ugly apartment building and the attractive one, even your chairs and your flowers and the figurines in your window bleached colorless by the sun, takes on a kind of transformed quality. For a moment you are in a parallel reality or a fairy tale, like you have traveled forward or backward in time. Everything is gold. No, everything is the color it is supposed to be, but more so. Even the ugliest thing is beautiful. Maybe it is something holy. But really, that's a kind of elevation, or even glorification. The moment passes and you aren't too sure you saw anything worth thinking twice about. You're that kind of person.

Sadland

YOUR BOYFRIEND HAS a conspicuous amount of sadness. He moves through his days in a blue fog, head hung, voice toneless and quiet, hands unnaturally soft. When you hold his hands it's like your hands might pass through his at any moment, they are so soft, soft as clouds, basically untouchable. Your boyfriend's sadness is visible but not touchable. You can see the sadness in his eyes and on his nose and cheeks and forehead, the planes of his chest, his hips and the dimples in his lower back, the curve of his heel, the calluses on his toes. Running your fingers along the landscapes of his body you can say, there's your sadness, and there, and there.

Even as sad as he is your boyfriend gets up in the morning, does the things he's always done. He makes pancakes for breakfast but doesn't eat any. He picks up around the house, takes the dog out for a walk, gives tennis lessons to local teens. He works out but he doesn't enjoy it. He works out because working out makes him less sad than he is the rest of the time, but he is still very sad, almost immeasurably sad. That's what he tells you, when every day you ask him how his sadness is doing. You ask him how his sadness is and he tells you it's the same, that he is immeasurably sad.

You ask him at what times he is more or less sad. You make a very detailed chart of where his sadness is at any point in a given day. You make note of the things that make him more sad or less sad. You measure out his immeasurable sadness in the lines and color-coding in your sadness chart.

You are not sad, or not very sad. You are no sadder or less sad than anyone else, so that when you walk down the street you can look at the faces of people who are walking the other way, and you can say that person is exactly as sad as I am. Really, there is so much to be sad about, small things that make you briefly sad, like when you watch the news or see a homeless person on the street or hear about a friend who lost a baby, but then your day moves on and you feel less sad and at the end of the day you tuck yourself snugly under the covers next to your boyfriend and none of that sadness stays with you. The only sadness in your bed is your boyfriend's sadness, the sadness you are used to. For all your charts and analysis, you aren't sure why your boyfriend is any sadder than anyone else, why he is so much sadder than you are. He has, for example, a life exactly as comfortable as your life. When you ask him if he is saddened by, perhaps, the state of the world, events overseas, the war, the other war, some natural disaster or another, he shakes his head at you. I'm not sad about any of that.

It's true that according to your chart, your boyfriend is not sadder when there is a suicide bombing, and he is not any less sad on days when you go together down to the lake and hike the trail through the hills all the way around, which he always says is his favorite thing to do with you.

Some days your boyfriend is so sad that he can't do anything, he stays in bed with the covers up around him and the lights dim and sometimes he is silent and other times he cries a little, quietly. You try to leave him alone on those days, coming in only to check on him, sit on the edge of the bed and place your hand on the lump of him under the covers. You don't ask are you okay because he hates being asked that. You let him know you're there.

Eventually there comes a time when your boyfriend doesn't get out of bed for a very long time, days and then weeks. You are worried, troubled that he has given up, but also a little frustrated, because you don't know what to do for him when everything you do seems like not quite enough. On your chart you circle the dates and make an annotation—critical mass!?—and your boyfriend's sadness goes on unchanging, no matter how many times you bring him happy news, no matter how many times the dog comes into the room and places his wet nose on the mattress next to your boyfriend's face. Your boyfriend loves the dog, but he does not get out of bed, he does not remove from his sadness.

Eventually, his sadness removes from him. You wake up one morning and although your boyfriend is still in bed, you hear sounds from the bathroom, and you find his sadness brushing its teeth, styling its hair, rubbing your boyfriend's restorative lotions into the lines of its face. It doesn't say anything or acknowledge your presence, your boyfriend's sadness, just goes about its version of your boyfriend's exact morning routine in silence, and slowly, with an exaggerated slowness like it is moving through the steps of some kind of dance.

Your boyfriend's sadness looks exactly like your boyfriend but sadder, with a kind of blueness about the face and hands like someone who has been deprived of oxygen for too long, or has been exposed to a nearly lethal dose of cold. You look harder at your boyfriend's sadness, but the physical differences are subtle, maybe your boyfriend's sadness has fingers that are too long, or a slightly crooked nose, or thinner lips, but you can't really tell. The main difference is in the sadness' eyes, ringed with dark circles, eyelids low, pupils black and huge, so large that your boyfriend's sadness doesn't seem to even have an eye color.

The sadness turns around and walks through you like you are nothing, passes through leaving only a fine mist on your skin where it touched you. When you are in contact with your boyfriend's sadness, you also become very sad, and you understand what it means to be possessed of an immeasurable sadness. You understand finally that this is a sadness that cannot be mapped or charted, cannot be rendered graphically or numerically or in terms of world events or babies lost. When your boyfriend's sadness leaves, away to the kitchen to make its sad pancakes, you expect your own sadness to lift, but it doesn't, you are still immeasurably sad.

You live a sad life with your boyfriend's sadness. It disappears at night while your boyfriend is asleep, but otherwise, the sadness does the things your boyfriend did. Somehow it makes pancakes and gives tennis lessons and goes to the gym and walks the dog, does all the things your boyfriend did, but sadder and sadder still. Everyone who is around your boyfriend's sadness becomes sadder. The dog droops its little head. The other people at the gym move a little slower, lose all or most of their pep. The local teens start to wear all black, dye their hair, write poetry, they are so sad. You are sad while you eat pancakes and find the act of eating the pancakes to also be sad, the pancakes make you even sadder.

Soon you spend more and more time with your boyfriend in bed. You spoon him and talk into his ear. He mumbles things back. You are both exactly as sad as each other. You thought your boyfriend would become un-sad after a period of separation from his sadness, but if anything, he has become sadder. You understand, as your sadness is also becoming sadder, more profound. More unescapable, more incalculable, every day. Eventually the dog joins you, lays on the bed between you and your boyfriend. The dog is also immeasurably sad, probably, although the dog has always had a sad face anyway, one of those droopy-faced dogs, so it could be sad or maybe it is just being a dog, or maybe it is just pleased to be allowed on the bed. But no, you look the dog in its droopy face and it seems sad to you, no question.

One morning you wake up but you don't get out of bed, and your sadness gets out of bed instead. It joins your boyfriend's sadness in the bathroom, does all of your usual morning bathroom things. The dog's sadness is there too, and all three together look cold and blue and oxygen-starved, but normal. You realize that they are a matched set and their sadness makes them well-suited for each other. They don't pass through each other like clouds, when they touch, their hands make contact, skin gives a little. They are a sad family, a family of sadness. Nobody makes a chart because nobody needs to, and from bed you think that it is better, that maybe your sadnesses, as a group, can make more sense of each other than you could. They have no charts.

What a sad life, you think, planting your forehead in the curve of your boyfriend's neck, unable to hold your head up any longer. The dog stirs, makes a gruff little noise and shifts his bulk a little bit, gets comfortable in the space between your legs and your boyfriend's. I love spending the day with you, you mumble into your boyfriend's shoulder, and he says yes, yes. You are both pretty sad, but slowly you are becoming somewhat happy about it.

Your sadness takes your boyfriend's sadness out to the lake that day, with the dog's sadness and a picnic, and they walk through the hills all the way around, and in the sunlight they seem less blue, less cold, more breathing, less sad. They sit on a blanket and eat fruit and cheese and wine, just like you and your boyfriend might have done. Your sadness and your boyfriend's sadness and your dog's sadness have a perfect day together. They throw a sad Frisbee for the dog, take sad pictures of the lake with their phones, hold their sad hands. The whole scene is very sad, and the whole world, too.

Jane Eyre

YOU DISCOVER THAT when you cut off your boyfriend's arm he grows a new arm. You examine the newly grown arm, and find it is exactly the same as the old arm, no better or worse. Under scrutiny, it doesn't even seem to be any newer. Just a regular boyfriend arm, the kind your boyfriend has, the arm you're used to. The cut-off arm is also no different. You hold them near each other and cannot tell them apart.

The room where you lock up your boyfriend is wood with a dirt floor. Really it's less like a room and more like a shed. You keep your boyfriend in the shed while you work on studying his amazing re-growing limbs. You do the difficult work of sawing through your boyfriend's skin and muscle and bone. The bone is the hardest, it takes the longest. It's a pain, it's definitely a pain. You give your boyfriend a leather wallet to bite down on. This is going to hurt, you say. You dare not use anesthetic in case it negatively affects your boyfriend's regenerative properties.

You suspend the cut-off limbs in scientific fluids to see if you can encourage them to grow a new boyfriend. You try to determine the very smallest piece that your boyfriend will re-grow from. But the limbs suspended in scientific fluid are pristine, unchanged. They still do all their usual things—the fingernails grow and the skin cells slough off and replenish. Regular arm stuff. But the jagged wound at the shoulder doesn't heal and no matter what you do you can't encourage it to grow another boyfriend.

Ultimately you wind up with so many spare boyfriend parts you could make an entire second boyfriend if you cut off a few more things, so you cut off a few more things. At this point you are an expert, you have the sharpest tools, your dissections are clean and even and painless. Your boyfriend barely makes a sound. You stitch together all the parts you have, the arms and legs and torso and butt. Even a head. Your boyfriend even re-grew his head. When you stitch the head onto the body (tiny, perfect sutures, almost invisible) the second boyfriend opens his eyes and looks around. Right away he makes inarticulate sounds, a strange howling.

Now that you have a second boyfriend, you're not sure what to do with him. You decide he should sit in the shed with your first boyfriend, who spends his days on the cot staring at a wall. The second boyfriend curls into himself in the corner, sits in the dirt and hugs his knees. When you shut the door, he starts crying, sobbing really, and doesn't stop. You think it's the second boyfriend who is crying. The next day you come to check on your boyfriend and your other boyfriend, and they have your tools, and they are cutting off their own limbs, cutting off each other's limbs, but they just re-grow, everything they cut away grows back, and both of them are crying and when you hold them near each other you can't tell them apart.

Bump in the Night

YOUR HOUSE IS very noisy at night, and your boyfriend decides he is going to fix it because he can't tolerate noise while he's trying to sleep. He believes that it is your plumbing that has been keeping him awake, and he opens up your toilet tank and replaces everything inside with new valves and pumps, all shiny and clean and modern-looking. When that doesn't stop the noise, he goes into your walls, pulls out old pipes and replaces them with new pipes. He still hears noises at night. He replaces your sink, your faucet, your hot water heater. He replaces your septic tank with a new septic tank. He can't find the source of the noise. He's up at all hours of the night, shaking you awake. Do you hear that?

He replaces all the wood flooring in case it creaks. He replaces the window glass. He replaces all of the fire alarms. He throws out the radios, the televisions, the computers, the alarm clocks, the grandfather clocks. He unplugs the refrigerator, the dishwasher, the ice maker, the stove.

He becomes convinced that you are the reason he can't sleep, and he replaces you. Maybe he sleeps better, finally, but you aren't sure. You stand out on the curb, it's about dusk, and everything is so quiet. You can't hear anything. You look at the house you used to live in, but you don't recognize it. The walls are gone, the yard has been dug up. There's nothing left but the studs and the dirt and your boyfriend, tossing and turning in his bed. Next to him is a shape that should be you, still and silent, not breathing. The new copper pipes gleam greasy orange from the streetlight. You don't know whose house it is, but it's not your house.

You stand on the sidewalk with your suitcase in one hand. That's not my house, you think, laughing as loud as you can.

Responsible Ownership

YOUR BOYFRIEND ADOPTS a pet without asking you about it first. You should have called me, you say. Your boyfriend tells you that he found the pet by the side of the road. I don't think we're ready for a pet, you say.

You and your boyfriend are not ready for a pet. One day you realize that the pet's water dish has been empty and you don't know for how long. The pet looks at you with its big eyes and it makes you feel bad. You're late to work that day. Your boyfriend never remembers to feed the pet and when you confront him about it he says it was your turn to feed the pet. It wasn't your turn, and you make a chart about whose turn it is to feed the pet so this doesn't happen again, but the chart disappears. Your boyfriend says the pet ate it, but the pet is so skinny you don't believe it.

You reluctantly take responsibility for the pet. You take it outside to go to the bathroom, you teach it tricks, you give it treats, and you play with it to make sure it gets exercise. You give it baths, covering your eyes with your hand because you feel uncomfortable watching it bathe. Once, you think you catch it watching from the door while you and your boyfriend are having sex, but when you get up to check, it's not there.

Over time, your efforts at caring for the pet never seem more than perfunctory. You'd hoped this would be a rewarding experience but mostly you find the pet incredibly boring. It's not the pet's fault, you remind yourself, and try to keep an open mind about it. But you can't help finding the pet tedious. All it does is cry and ask where its parents are, and you keep saying, I don't know, I don't know.

The Blood Mouth

YOU MOVE WITH your boyfriend to the desert. Initially this seems like a bad idea, but as you're driving across the cracked earth, the cracked road, the cracks in the road and the earth and your hands filling with dust, you realize this is the worst fucking idea anyone has ever had. This idea is so bad you choke on it, or you think that you choke on it, you stop the car, you spit and your spit is mud. You expect the ground to drink up the moisture, you expect the ground to be thirsty, but really the glob of dust and spit sits on the surface of the desert like a bubble until it evaporates.

Your boyfriend gets the blood mouth almost immediately. The desert town has an Old West Doctor. He carries a battered leather bag like in the movies. He has a black stethoscope around his neck. He wears a tweed vest and a striped long-sleeved shirt with stains in the pits. I'm trying to live as much like an Old West Doctor as I can, the Old West Doctor tells you, conversationally. I feel like it's a more authentic medicine.

While the Old West Doctor tells you this, your boyfriend is bleeding from the mouth, or is spitting up a blood-like substance, a thick crimson sludge he catches in a metal bowl. Your landlady smelled the coppery stench when she came by asking about the rent. She told you it's the blood mouth and you should call the Old West Doctor. He's an asshole, she said, and while this should have felt like she was inviting you into a confidence, something about the way she said it made it seem the opposite. You gave her the rent and called the doctor.

Old West medicine isn't much, you think, after the doctor takes a look at your boyfriend and takes a look at the bloodsludge, almost black where it's congealed in the bowl. He takes a little bit of the blood and rubs it between his fingers. It looks like he's asking for a tip. Your boyfriend's bottom lip is a high-gloss red. He became pale and thin almost immediately after he started leaking blood from his mouth. It was his idea to move here, you remind yourself, but now you look at him all sexy and bearded and dying, and it's hard to hold anything against him. You take his blood mouth bowl out to rinse while he talks to the Old West Doctor.

When your boyfriend asked you to consider moving to the desert you assumed water would be dear, but the people who live in the desert town throw it away casually. People take showers three, sometimes four times a day. The streets are lined with troughs of water for thirsty animals to drink from. Every square has a fountain, and all of the fountains run all night. The town has a greenhouse where a sophisticated irrigation system rains a month's worth of water down on a flourishing rainforest ecosystem several times a day. You went to the greenhouse once and found it an almost hallucinatory experience, so hot it felt like you'd caught a fever. As water rained down from the sky you sat on a bench and pretended you were dying of dysentery.

You contemplated stripping down to your underwear and standing greasy and wet under the trees, feeling the heat and water directly on your skin. Instead you slicked your hair back and felt the water drip down your neck and between your shoulder blades. Hot as blood.

You rinse out your boyfriend's metal bowl with a few pumps from the old cast iron water pump outside. It's tremendous overkill, the rush of water thinning the almost-black blood to a winsome pinkish color before washing it away. You're standing in a mudhole before you know it. The bowl never comes quite clean; on the inside is a wide black mark that doesn't wash out, the discolored stainless steel gritty to the touch. You scratch at it with your fingernails but can't get the stain to lift. Once, you used the bowl for mixing cake batter, blending eggs for omelets or swirling vegetables around in olive oil. Now, to think of it having once contained food makes you ill.

Since coming to the desert you feel exhausted and sexual. You feel like you have been drunk since noon. You feel like you are at the end of the party, like it is two in the morning and a boy is following you around and you know that he's in love with you and it would be easy. Since you left the greenhouse that stripped-down-and-slick feeling hasn't gone away. You pass the Old West Doctor, who is just leaving your home, and you try to wedge him into a sexual fantasy, you try to make yourself want him. It doesn't work. You don't want him. You are angry that he left your boyfriend alone. You are angry he didn't wait to give you an update. You are angry with yourself for not staying, for going out to wash the bowl. You could have washed the bowl anytime.

When you get the bowl back to your boyfriend, he looks relieved, you think to see you, but immediately he leans forward and releases the mouthful of blood he had been holding into the bowl. It isn't thick and sludgy this time, it gushes and splashes, maybe because he's been holding on to it for too long. It runs down the sides of the bowl like water.

Your boyfriend's condition keeps you near the house. You tell yourself that it is your boyfriend's condition. Really you are walking around in a state of constant arousal. You don't want to be too far away from your boyfriend in case he wakes up and suddenly feels capable. While he is asleep, you take showers, the water as hot as you can stand. Once, you turn on the shower while you are still fully clothed and remove your drenched clothing one article at a time. Afterwards, you can't bring yourself to put new clothing on. You walk around the house naked. This does something for you, but not enough, so you open the doors and windows, let the air and heat in. Your wet clothes remain at the bottom of the shower and dry into strange, stiff shapes.

Your body has changed since you came to the desert town. You remember feeling dissatisfied with your disappointing body before, the sagging inner tube of fat around your midsection, the marshmallows of your upper arms. Mostly your body felt too heavy, like you were sagging, bouncing, dragging along. In the desert your body is like someone else's. It is lean and controlled. Nothing bounces. You are all clean lines and tight, geometrical shapes. You no longer lament that you are not fit or attractive. You feel incredibly fit and attractive. Your body is a powerhouse, but you don't feel strong. Instead, you are full of energy, brimming over, barely contained, but fragile. Like a glass jar that could easily break and spill its contents.

You spend much of the day pacing the house, walking to the living room, the bathroom, the small, dark room you use as an office, the bedroom where your boyfriend sleeps. You repeat a circle around the inside of the house. You pass every open door and window, where you would be visible to any passers-by, although frustratingly, there are none. You stop in the bedroom, sit on the bed next to your boyfriend. You are not gentle. You rock the bed hoping to wake him up. You touch him, his face, his shoulders, his chest. You pretend that your hands are careful, clinical and precise, taking measurements, assessing health, but really you are groping at him sloppily. Your hands are paws. They are damp and swollen. You hope he will wake up, but instead you hear the landlady walk up the path and knock.

Rent's due, the landlady says, and if she registers that you are naked, she says nothing. It is sweltering in your house, you are sweating so profusely that your feet slip on the floor. The landlady doesn't come inside.

I just paid the rent, you say.

Been a month, the landlady says, rent's due.

You write out and hand her a damp check, the ink smeared from the wet edge of your palm. She takes it, with no comment, just folds it neatly down the center and slides it under the strap of her bra.

All this—your unapologetic nudity, the landlady's strange nonchalance, your boyfriend ill in the next room— should seem sexy, but it isn't. This is exactly a scene from a pornographic video, you think. You have watched many of them in your life. You tell yourself this scenario is hot, despite your body's objections, but you can't convince your-self, because it isn't. You're just too warm. For her part, the landlady seems similarly unimpressed with you, stands in the doorway waiting for you to say something.

Outside, clouds are gathering and you didn't realize how big the sky looked in the desert town until the clouds start-ed to make it seem squat, claustrophobic. There is a yellow quality to the light that is disconcerting to you. A wind has picked up and you can see little flurries of dust stirred up in the distance, gathering quickly, spinning, and falling again.

I should go back inside, you say, not to the landlady or anyone in particular. I should check on him.

The blood mouth, she says.

That's not his name, you say, but she has already started to walk away.

For the rest of the afternoon, you sit in a chair by your boyfriend's bedside. He wakes up occasionally, reaches for you, but by the time you reach back he has passed out again. You begin to worry about the amount of time he spends passed out. Then you envy him. You wonder what kinds of dreams he has.

It starts to rain, but it is still oppressive in the house. You put towels on the floor beneath the open windows to keep the rain from damaging the floors, although you don't real-ly know if it will do any good. The water collecting on the towels contributes a musty smell and an incredible amount of humidity. You wonder if this kind of heat is good for your boyfriend, but you don't know what else to do, you have not seen a single fan or air conditioner since you came to the desert town.

You watch your boyfriend lie still in the bed, occasionally leaning over to spit into the metal bowl. He is sweating and has kicked all the blankets off. You crawl into the bed with him, nestle his body in yours. He has gotten so small you can easily wrap your arm around his chest, pull his body into yours. You are holding this small, sweaty thing that you love, and soon you are uncomfortable because it's too hot to be this close to anyone. You let yourself sweat, you let him sweat, you both soak the sheet and the mattress protector and the mattress. Even though the roof is protecting you from the rain it suddenly feels like you and your boyfriend have been standing together in the downpour, both of you getting soaked and slick.

You are thinking about how much you want to be inside him. You are not sure if you mean this in a sexual way, although, sure, you can imagine entering him in the traditional way. You can imagine penetrating him. The way you imagine it, he is awake, and not just awake but eagerly awake, awake and kind and encouraging. Maybe he says yes to you a lot, maybe even asks politely, says please and thank you.

But more than that you want to be inside him in whatever other way you can. You want to open up his back and crawl inside, where it is hotter, unbearably hot and wet and bloody. You want his body to be your body and his thoughts to be your thoughts. You want to have everything be together, all jumbled up, both of you part of the same unruly mess, inseparable. You want uncomfortable closeness. You want to hold him so hard that you mush together, but no matter how you try the membrane separating you remains disappointingly impermeable.

Eventually you untangle from your boyfriend and go outside, where it is pouring so hard that your clothes immediately soak through and cling uncomfortably to your body. You are shocked to discover you are wearing clothes. You wonder if you've been wearing them this whole time. Looking at the clothes, they aren't familiar. You don't look like you. You don't recognize your fingernails or your knuckles or your palms or the chubby pads of your fingers. You don't recognize your wrists or your forearms, your chest or the gentle slope of your stomach.

Whose body is this, anyway, you wonder. Who am I?

Standing in the rain, you are reminded again of the greenhouse. You try to picture yourself there, but it seems so possible that you imagined it. Did you really leave your sick boyfriend alone to wander into town and look at plants? Is the desert town really full of water?

But the streets are filling like rivers and, at least for the moment, the desert town really is full of water, though you don't know where it all goes.

You check your body again. The feel of standing in it, walking in it. Nothing feels right. Maybe it's the rain, and you go back inside, drip water behind you on the floor.

Your boyfriend, still sleeping, looks more like you than you do, and you wonder if you've had it wrong the whole time, if you are actually your boyfriend and you are the one who has the blood mouth, the one lying in bed and, for all Old West medicine can do for you, dying. You try to imagine mourning yourself, preparing to live the rest of your life without yourself.

This seems preposterous to you. Yet, whoever you are, you are no one recognizable.

Here's what you do know:

You and your boyfriend met for the first time at a bar. You waited until the bar was closing, around two in the morning, and kissed him on the sidewalk outside. You wanted to make him wait around for you. It was so easy. You had both been waiting for you to get around to it. He was so eager it felt like he was already in love with you. It was raining but not cold. When you picture it, the person who was kissing your boyfriend was recognizably you. He had the body you were used to, the non-desert body. Your boyfriend was recognizably your boyfriend. You remember the smell of smoke, the sound of music from inside the bar, the girl screaming I love this song! and you remember thinking, yes, me too, I also love this song. This was the first time you remember trying to collapse your two bodies together. You kissed him so hard you cut his lip with your teeth. It bled enough that you could taste it.

VI

*The Game Begins to Occupy
a Very Central Place in Your Life*

Zombie Apocalypse Story

EVERYONE LOVES YOUR boyfriend. There was a time when you were proud of this, but then it got worse and eventually it was a huge problem. It started small. The neighbor would come over to talk to your boyfriend while you were at work. He would smile at your boyfriend. He would bring gifts. Eventually he stopped waiting for you to be at work, he would come over at all hours of the day and night to say hello to your boyfriend, to chat. Your boyfriend was polite but has never been very friendly. Eventually you would wake up in the morning to find the front porch covered in presents for your boyfriend, from the neighbor. Piles of gifts, all wrapped in beautiful paper, letters splashed with the most expensive cologne. A fragrant heap. One day you couldn't open the door. It's just a crush, your boyfriend said, but you couldn't even find the fucking garage when you got home from work. Then there were the dead animals. The neighbor would bring little dead animals and leave them on the porch for your boyfriend. Rats and squirrels and small birds. Then dogs and cats. Then humans, children and old people, then small adults, then that one coworker your boyfriend couldn't stand. You had to move.

You don't really get it, the way that everyone loves your boyfriend now. He's incredibly beautiful, yes, but not more so than any model on a runway or in a catalogue. His personality is what you would describe as fine. He has a good sense of humor but he's moody. He's kind-hearted but not especially friendly. Sometimes you spend the day looking at him, squinting your eyes this way and that, trying to figure it out and failing, utterly failing, because to you he's just your boyfriend. He wakes up with bad breath. He never does the dishes. He leaves his laundry in big piles on the sofa. He doesn't answer his phone, even in an emergency. He's a bad driver.

He's such a bad driver that when you go on the run he never drives, it's only you. After the neighbor incident, you both move across town, to a different house with different neighbors. After a day, the new neighbors, men, women, and children, surround your home in a thick circle of bodies. They are chanting your boyfriend's name, uttering declarations of love. They press their bodies against the exterior walls of your house and moan. Several times you wake in the middle of the night to hear hands clawing at the windows and doors. Parents try to shove their small children through your dog door so the children can unlock the house and let them in. At the darkest part of one night, you stumble into the kitchen and turn on the light to find a child stuck in the dog door, one shoulder dislocated so he will fit. He is thrashing against the confines of the door, drooling on the floor. I love your boyfriend, he says. I love your boyfriend so much.

You ask your boyfriend if there is anything he wants to tell you about this situation, but he just shrugs and says no.

He is upset that you disturbed him in the middle of the night when you know he does poorly on too little sleep. I find this behavior inconsiderate, he says.

The next morning you pretend that you are heading off to work like usual but you hide your boyfriend in the trunk of your car. After that you are on the run. You learn not to stop for cops, who only stop you to get to your boyfriend. You turn the car radio off after the radio stations stop playing music and instead dedicate themselves to your boyfriend, only your boyfriend, 24/7. I have not left the studio in six days, one radio announcer says. I have not eaten and I only pee in a jar. I just love your boyfriend so, so much. He concludes his broadcast by weeping and moaning and chanting your boyfriend's name, over and over. This is what being on the run is like. You have to hide your boyfriend under a pile of blankets when you get gas. It's too hot under here, he says, and you tell him to shut up.

Obviously this has strained your relationship with each other. He is always annoyed at having to hide and run and spend all day in the car. You are always annoyed that he is not taking this seriously enough. Sometimes, after a fight, he presses his lips together into a flat line and says, I could just leave and anyone I met would take me in and protect me and treasure me. You want to say, you have no fucking idea what these people would do to you, but instead you say, you're right. I probably like you less than anyone else in the world right now.

This is not, strictly speaking, the truth. You are annoyed with him, yes, but because he keeps making it so hard to keep him hidden and safe. You are trying to protect him. You are trying to make sure no one can take him away from you. Every morning, you drive down the road, watching over your shoulder for a caravan of cars coming to chase you down and steal him away. Sometimes your eye drifts over to your boyfriend, who has a bored expression on his face, his cheek resting on one hand, elbow propped up on the side panel of the car. He is so beautiful. You love him so much, so violently. There is nothing you wouldn't do for him. Still driving, you lean over to kiss his neck.

Manure

YOUR BOYFRIEND KIDNAPS all of the talking animals.
They had such a nice existence, before. The talking animals were friendly and enthusiastic. They danced and sang
and did stand-up comedy. They dispensed the most excellent advice, it was widely known that the talking animals
gave the best advice, always there with a shoulder to cry on
and a reasonable way out of a problem. They were deeply
anthropomorphic; many of them stood on their hind legs
and had opposable thumbs. The talking lions could open
a can of beer, the talking kangaroos could play ping-pong,
the talking dolphins were able masseurs. It was a happy
existence, just an incredibly happy way to live. You wished
you were a talking animal, in those days.

But your boyfriend is good at kidnapping, maybe too
good. He hunted the talking animals down, one by one. He
caught the talking bears, eating tuna sandwiches on their
lunch breaks, he caught the talking elephants at their tennis lessons, he caught the talking owls in their adult movie
theaters. Most of the talking animals he captured but some
of them he killed, because you only need so many talking
alligators before you have too many and he has limited
space. It's like a Noah's Ark thing, he says, but you fail to

see the logic in it, the odd numbers of animals, sometimes one or three or five in a cage, the fact that there is no reason for it, that there is no ark or biblical flood or need to repopulate the earth. That he keeps them underground in the dark. Really, you don't even know what he wants with them, certainly not conversation, not advice.

Life is as terrible for the captured talking animals as it was wonderful before. Your boyfriend is not kind to them. He takes away their clothes—their tiny animal pants!—and doesn't allow them access to their favorite reality shows. He keeps them in your very dark basement, and it is inadequately ventilated and your boyfriend is not conscientious about cleaning the cages, which are piled haphazardly one on top of the other, all the way to the ceiling. You shudder to think of it, as you spend your days reading on your window seat in the afternoon sun, eating poached eggs alone in your breakfast nook, tending to your beautiful garden. All that, while in your basement there are all those talking animals, most of them professionals, doctors and lawyers and scholars, weeping in their own filth, and when you imagine you can hear them you quickly raise the volume on your radio. You listen to Ira Glass interview a very old man who has had some trouble with a woodpecker attacking his house.

You know one thing for sure: all that talking animal poop is wonderful fertilizer for your garden. The rhododendrons are positively enchanting this year.

What Keeps Society Going

YOUR BOYFRIEND GIVES up and goes into The Business. He had been talking about it a lot lately, like one day you can't pay the power bill and your boyfriend mutters something about going into The Business, how much easier it would be if he just went into The Business. He won't leave it alone, The Business, bringing it up whenever he has an opening. My father was in The Business, he says, and our bills were always paid on time.

So fine, you say, Call your father. Go into The Business. Either do it or don't.

You expected your challenge to go un-answered but sure enough the next morning you wake up and your boyfriend is dressed like you would expect someone in The Business to dress. He looks alone and awkward in the clothes, like a little boy, and you love him through the feeling mounting in your chest that this is the beginning of some disaster you have already completely lost control of. You do your usual morning things, brew a cup of tea, rub lotion into your hands, let the cat out. In the backyard, you chop some wood, run a mile, check on the goats. You go about your morning and you assume that your boyfriend has already gone off to work, gone off to The Business, but when you get back to the house after all that, he is still standing there, eyes vague.

I start tomorrow, he says.

He stands in much this same fashion all through the afternoon and evening and into the night. You do the things you usually do. Before he went into The Business, your boyfriend was out of the house during the day. You don't know what he did, exactly, you assumed that maybe he did a lot of drinking and a lot of gambling to pay for the drinking, or maybe he stole cars or purses, but you've always liked terrible men and so you imagine that your boyfriend is of course up to no good, and the fantasy of him being up to no good is largely what has sustained you throughout your relationship, and with all that being said, you are unprepared for the fact that he has become furniture.

You get ready for bed. You brush and floss your teeth, and wash your hair, and file your fingernails until their edges are soft, and rub lotion into your elbows and knees, and put out fresh food and water for the cat. The whole time your boyfriend stands there, in his clothes for The Business, and you don't even know where he got those clothes for The Business, certainly not in this house, certainly not from you. In fact, you haven't paid a second of attention to The Business in your entire life, you know about it, of course, everyone knows The Business is what keeps society going, but you've never had anything to do with any of that. You are not invested in whatever it is that keeps society going, and, come to think of it, neither is your boyfriend, or at least you feel fairly certain your boyfriend is not invested in keeping society going, turning gears or the wheels of progress or sprocket factories or anything of that nature.

Are you coming to bed? you ask him.

I am waiting for a call, he says, this is how The Business works.

The call never comes, or if it does it comes while you are asleep and therefore don't notice it or care very much about it. In the morning you hear him make a cup of coffee and start the car and leave. You don't hear him shower or change his clothes or make a phone call or brush his teeth. You don't hear him let the cat out. That makes sense, as those things are your job, and so since you're awake anyway, you shower and change your clothes and make a phone call and brush your teeth and let the cat out. You feel very supportive, doing these important things so your boyfriend can focus on The Business.

You try to imagine him in The Business but your imagination can't fill in the gaps, can't quite make anything out of how little you know about The Business, and instead you imagine him doing other things. For example, you imagine him robbing a bank, or stealing a car, or sticking a knife in another man wearing the costume of The Business. Perhaps stealing the knifed man's watch and wallet and keys. Or, you imagine your boyfriend is performing some kind of espionage, that he has entered The Business in order to steal all of its secrets and sell them to the highest bidder. Or maybe he plans to release all of the secrets of The Business on a free website that everyone will access so they will know everything about The Business and the mysterious ways in which it keeps society going. You imagine that your boyfriend has gone too deeply into The Business and has trouble remembering who is friend and who is foe, and then he is discovered in his espionage by a boyishly handsome man who is also in The Business but is sympathetic to your boyfriend's intentions, whether he is working for personal financial gain or socially-responsible altruism. Your boyfriend has trouble trusting the idealistic young man from The Business, but eventually they become lovers and vow to take down The Business together.

In your fantasies, you are the person paying your boyfriend fifty million dollars for all of the secrets of The Business, or you are the open-minded tech entrepreneur who supports your boyfriend's free website of secrets. Sometimes you are the person sitting at home scrolling through the secrets of The Business on the free website your boyfriend and the open-minded tech entrepreneur built and you can feel through the layers of the fantasy that the secrets of The Business are important but fundamentally boring. You are reminded why you don't care very much what keeps society going.

Sometimes in your fantasies you are an ambitious young security guard who catches your boyfriend and his lover in their espionage. Sometimes you let them go, confident that The Business will no longer have any power over you after they destroy it, but in most of the fantasies you shoot them both to death. You point your gun at them and scream that they should kiss, they should kiss each other, like they mean it, and then while they are kissing you shoot them, you shoot them a lot, until they are very dead and also full of bullets.

Does the human body get heavier after it is shot up, you wonder? You like to imagine the bullets weigh a lot.

Because you believe your boyfriend is on an important mission to bring The Business down, you begin to help him in any way that you can. When he comes home at night and stands perfectly still and doesn't move, you remove the clothes he put on for The Business and you replace them with other clothes that he can also wear to The Business. You dry-clean the other clothes from The Business so that your boyfriend always has something fresh to wear. You scrub him, too, just scrub him everywhere, make sure that he is clean and pink and ready for The Business. You rub lotion into his hands and elbows and knees so that his skin is soft and appropriate-looking. You give him protein shakes, for nourishment, and you find if you tilt his head just right, you can pour the protein shakes right down his throat even if he refuses to swallow. You discover that if you make the protein shakes coffee-flavored, he'll drink them willingly, so you do that.

Helping your boyfriend commit espionage begins to take its toll on you. Because you have dedicated so much energy to helping your boyfriend succeed in his mission, you are not doing very basic tasks around your home, like rubbing lotion into your skin or letting the cat in or checking on the goats. The cat has been loose outside for god knows how long. Maybe the cat finally got hungry enough that he ate the goats. You regret that you let something bad happen to the goats, although it seems better than something happening to the cat. Your teeth remain unbrushed and you remain unshowered while your boyfriend goes to The Business every morning and comes home every night to stand very still in a single spot in the home that you share. When he is at The Business, you take your turn standing very still in the exact spot that your boyfriend stands when it's his turn to stand very still.

Your skin gets so dirty and dry that it turns red, and then it begins to itch and peel and you break out in strange scaly patches that cover your entire body. You look like a terrifying lizard-person and you smell horrible, although your boyfriend doesn't notice either of those things when he comes home to stand very still on the floor. Many weeks pass and you don't notice any espionage happening. You get bored standing very still in one place in your house. Eventually you stop standing very still in one place and check the internet for secrets about The Business and find that there aren't any. Your boyfriend has not succeeded in his mission, or perhaps he is not trying and you only imagined that part. According to the internet, The Business is doing well, or terribly, and there are not enough people in The Business but there are too many people trying to get into The Business.

After much digging, you find a site that says the thing that really keeps society going is a secret cabal of lizard people who only want you to believe The Business is working, but it's all a sham because what the lizard people really like is control. You look in the mirror and realize you do look like a terrible lizard-person who might be part of some kind of secret cabal. There is something around the eyes and the corners of your mouth that suggests the tendency toward secrecy and even a little hint of the capacity for manipulation. You have the lizard-face of a lizard-person who really likes secretly controlling world events.

You decide to leave your home to find the other lizard people, who will sympathize with your situation and include you in their plan to control the world. Outside, you are joined by the cat, who looks sleek and well-fed on goat, and you sentimentally declare him an honorary lizard-person. The cat joins you on your journey to find the other lizard-people, who you hope will not eat him.

When your boyfriend comes home that night, to stand very still in a single spot and stare at a fixed point on the wall, you are not there to dress him and feed him and clean him, and while he doesn't seem to notice or alter his routine in any way, the next day he is a part of The Business that is functioning a little more poorly than the other parts, and every day after that, a little more poorly than before. Your house is slowly reclaimed by the landscape, your boyfriend coming home to floors covered in dirt, the power bill goes unpaid. The roof disappears one day, boom, no roof, just like that. Your boyfriend stands in the sun all weekend and afterward works in The Business with leathery skin, his Business costume faded to a dusty no-color. In the room where he stands, there is now a cactus, so he stands next to the cactus. The goats come inside, track their small hoof prints through the dirt, eat bits of the cactus and hallucinate because of the cactus juice. Your boyfriend stands next to the cactus and the hallucinating goats every night. He leaves for The Business every day. The goats see bizarre shapes and colors, the walls melting, an unfamiliar sky, they hear alien music. They stand still, all day, not moving a hoof, not even to get water, only occasionally stretching out their necks to bite off another bit of cactus. They don't move, though whether it's from fear or wonder is impossible to tell.

Spy vs. Spy

YOU BEGIN TO suspect your boyfriend might be cheating on you. There isn't any one thing, you don't catch him red-handed, don't find any sexual text messages or smell any strange cologne, it's just a nagging feeling you get that you can't ignore. He has, for example, started going to the gym more often. He is always at the gym. You recently read an article that said that 25% of people are having sex at the gym. Statistically, there's a 25% chance your boyfriend has been having sex at the gym, and if he has, it wasn't with you. You are never at the gym. You conclude that, at least, there is a 25% chance that your boyfriend is cheating on you.

You spend a lot of time convincing yourself that your boyfriend isn't cheating on you or that he is. You write in to Dear Prudie. You go on the Wendy Williams show. You read women's magazines and men's magazines. You ask some of your friends, all of whom are recently divorced. You sit with one of the recently divorced friends, the one with the perfect manicure, and you paint your nails together and drink strawberry daiquiris. She is recently divorced and mean about it. Not angry or bitter, mean. She keeps calling you girlfriend and laughing too loud. She is painting her nails acid green. She is making lewd comments about the young man who cleans her pool.

I am having sex at the gym, she tells you. Your boyfriend is probably having sex at the gym. I wouldn't be surprised. I mean, would you be surprised?

Talking to your mean divorced friend convinces you that your boyfriend is cheating on you and you decide the only thing to do about it is murder him. You talked a lot about that, when you first started seeing each other and everything was new and romantic. One night you lay back in the bed of your boyfriend's truck looking at the stars with your arm around his shoulder.

I hope we are always like this, you said. Romantic and in love with each other.

If I ever do anything to hurt you or our relationship, he said, you should absolutely murder me.

You remember it very clearly, him saying that.

Now you've decided to take him at his word. It's important, you think, to be consistent. Which is to say, when someone in a relationship makes a promise, they should keep it. You've always felt this way. You've always been a little strict, a little serious, a little self-righteous. When you were young you were not the one anyone wanted to hang out with. Your younger brother was always loose and charming, fun to be around and quick with a joke. You were responsible, dedicated, somber. Nobody wanted to be around you. Later your brother got addicted to drugs and you got your boyfriend. You tried to be fun and loose and charming. You made some friends, and later those friends got married and you didn't see them for a while. Now, they arc all getting divorced, and you once again feel like you have friends.

You think about ways to kill your boyfriend. You want it to look like a crime of passion. Not only because you know you will serve less jail time if you're caught, but because you want everyone to think you are capable of passion. Wow, they will say. After all this time, turns out he was really pretty passionate. Wow, we sure had him all wrong.

You start leaving deadly objects sitting around the house, at an arm's reach. Letter openers, heavy paperweights, odd decorative statues with sharp edges, kitchen knives, cuticle scissors, wooden lamps, iron candlesticks, toolboxes full of dangerous tools. You want to get in an argument with your boyfriend and then you want to murder him. This would be the ideal way for things to go. But time passes and you don't ever have quite the right argument. He fusses at you for keeping the house too warm, and you want to fight about that, but then you imagine stabbing your boyfriend because he has unreasonable expectations about temperature and honestly that just seems silly. Later you yell at him because he got 1% milk, which you hate, instead of 2% milk, which you love. You look at his face very closely and decide you don't want to murder this man you love because of milk.

You want to murder this man you love because he is cheating on you. Eyes on the prize, you tell yourself. Don't forget why we're doing this.

You practice wanting to murder him, just to see how it will feel once you finally get to it. One morning you hit your boyfriend with your car, experimentally, just to see how he looks sprawled out on the ground. You dent the car and break his leg, but he lives.

After the incident with the car and the broken leg, things around your house become tense and suspicious.

Your boyfriend starts to notice how there are deadly objects always within reach, and you notice him watching you. You have more fights, and during those fights your boyfriend stays carefully out of striking range. One night, not long after the incident with the car and the broken leg, your boyfriend knocks a bookcase over on you. He says it was a mistake, that he tripped and fell on one of his crutches. But you know the truth. You saw him wait for you to pass.

When the bookcase falls on you, you break a few ribs and dislocate your shoulder. You have to wear a sling. This is going to make it harder to murder your boyfriend, but not impossible. You feel very dedicated now. You are reverting to your old self, serious and responsible. If you are going to kill your boyfriend, you're going to do it right.

What follows is several weeks in which you and your boyfriend are very seriously trying to kill each other. Your boyfriend stops going to the gym. You stop going to work. You are both concentrating very hard on the murders. Around each other, you are very careful to focus on your routines. You do the things you usually do, eat dinner and watch movies and take long walks. You become aggressively romantic with each other in order to stay always in arm's reach, to remove the element of surprise. You have the most sex you've ever had in your life, incredibly violent sex, with some punching and stabbing and clubbing each other with lead pipes, which both of you loudly assure the other is the best sex you've ever had, this rough play is exactly what you've always wanted, don't stop. Afterward neither of you wants to fall asleep first. Instead you have long talks, learning things about each other, each of you trying to search out a fatal weakness.

Your boyfriend leaves a loose cobra in your closet. A gift, he knows you like animals.

You pour lube all over the bottom of his shower. An accident, you just used too much.

He shoots you in the back. He thought you a home invader.

You poison his dinner. You're incredibly clumsy in the kitchen.

He chokes you in your sleep. He was having a nightmare.

You electrocute him. You heard that was fun in the bedroom.

He throws acid at your face. He heard that was fun in the bedroom.

You hit him with an axe. You love him.

He pushes you into the oven. He loves you.

You lock him in a freezer. You love him more.

He sets a bomb under the cushion of your favorite chair. He loves you the most.

Eventually you are both so weak from poison and cobra venom and frostbite and burns and acid and axe wounds and explosions that you have to stop trying to kill each other. You have both been badly wounded but neither of you have died. You are under investigation by the police because you have made so many emergency calls but have both refused to press charges. Your neighbors hate you because of that time you cut the power lines and tried to drop the live wires on your boyfriend as he jogged by, the resulting power outage, and also because they are uncomfortable living next to the place where the bomb went off. The insurance company has begun to dispute your claims, which are extensive (the cure for the poison alone was ruinously expensive). Your divorced friends have stopped calling you because you seem too serious, because you're spending so much time with your boyfriend and it makes them feel bad, like you are not very fun anymore.

One night, you and your boyfriend sit in your wheelchairs on the deck, watching the stars and holding hands. You are both in a moderate amount of pain, your face still sore from the reconstructive surgery after the acid, his nerves still tingling from the electricity (or the cold? Or the poison? He isn't sure).

I hope I don't die from my wounds before I kill you, you say.

I've never wanted to kill anyone as much as I want to kill you, he says.

Fuck Marry Kill

You and your boyfriend play a lot of games of fuck, marry, kill. You're not sure where it started, whether it was you or him that proposed the first scenario—kill seems like you, fuck seems like him, marry seems like neither of you. In fact, when you play, you and your boyfriend play with adjustments to the traditional rules, and your rules almost never involve an option to marry. You play variants on the traditional scenarios, like kill kill fuck or fuck kill fuck or kill kill kill. Initially, you choose celebrities for the game. Tom Hiddleston, Christina Aguilera, Tilda Swinton. Who would you fuck and kill and fuck?

As you get to know each other better you play a trickier version of the game, involving close friends and loved ones. The idea is to create an untenable situation, where you are fucking and killing people you are reluctant to kill or fuck. Your mom, your best friend, your childhood pet. Kill fuck kill. There are uncomfortable contortions involved. Your boyfriend is actually much better at it than you are, or maybe you wind up going easy on him, while he grants no mercy to you. Either way, it is usually you who is boxed into a corner, forced to make an unhappy face and say, fuck,

I guess? and you both know that you don't really want to fuck your childhood pet or kill your mom.

The game begins to occupy a very central place in your life with your boyfriend. It is sometimes foreplay, sometimes amusement, and sometimes the stakes become very high. Your boyfriend uses it to ferret the truth out of you, who you're attracted to, who you hate. The only rule you both play by, unspoken but long agreed to, is that neither of you are allowed to put yourself in the game. In a relationship there is knowing the truth, and then there is knowing too much of the truth. You and your boyfriend are in love, and as such, you are both afraid to know too much of the truth. You are both very fragile, prone to hurt feelings and miscommunication. You could not say kill, even as a joke, about one another. You could not say fuck because it implies something, a transience maybe, or a casualness neither of you feel, and either of you would be hurt if the other said fuck about your life together, about your stupid collection of vintage troll dolls that started as a joke but now has become something very earnest, about the agreement you made with each other when you got rid of your mismatched old furniture and replaced it with new furniture you bought together, a matched set. Of course neither of you can say marry, either.

When the game gets too dull, you introduce new rules to keep it fresh. For example, you ban groups of people or limit yourselves to groups of people or forbid people entirely. Sometimes you are standing on the street waiting for a cab and you decide you'll play a quick game, just on the street. The man in the white cap, the woman in the green dress, the old lady with the cloth grocery bag that looks too heavy for her. Kill, fuck, kill. You can't kill the woman with the green dress because she's holding her daughter's hand. You can't kill the old lady because she's very old, has probably lived a long life, and she deserves to go out with some dignity, with some peace, like maybe she should fall asleep and just never wake up again. In other words, you aren't willing to kill an old lady. On the other hand, the man in the white cap is incredibly handsome, tall but not too tall, bearded but not too bearded, muscular but not too muscular. He is exactly enough, and you could imagine fucking him just because, and now you could fuck him to save his life, but then you have elected to murder a young mother (single, you decide, something about her tells you she's raising her little girl alone) or an old lady who has lived a long life (and difficult, you think, probably very difficult, she looks tired even for her age).

Still. Fuck, you say, pointing to the man in the white cap, which is what your boyfriend was trying to get you to admit to in the first place. Kill, you say, pointing to the young mother, and kill, you say, pointing to the old woman with the grocery bag.

Predictable, your boyfriend says, and he laughs at you. You are so predictable, he says again.

You made the choices too easy, you say, and anyway it's not like anyone really has to die. It's just a game.

Eventually your boyfriend has the idea: maybe more than just a game. He pulls up three profiles on your Facebook page, people who you know but who are not particularly important to you, but people who have occupied some space in your life. One is a casual acquaintance who you see fairly often, one you knew very well but a very long time ago, and one is a business contact you have never met in person, or only met once, in passing, but who has been helpful in your career.

Fuck fuck kill, your boyfriend says. For real this time.

Well, all three are passably fuckable. None of them present you with the desire to fuck that is so intense that it would save their lives by default. On the other hand, none of them are so deeply flawed that you think immediately that it would be fine to kill them, that you would be okay doing that so as to avoid fucking them, or because they seemed to deserve it. You do your math, like you are still playing the game in the usual way, because you always took it at least a little seriously.

The business contact is single, but he is very fit and gives a lot of money to charity, you see from his Facebook page, where it lists the charity marathons he has run in and the charity benefits he has attended. This combination between fitness and philanthropy makes him stand out, briefly, as more fuckable.

The casual acquaintance is married, but you don't like his wife, so you could fuck him or kill him and not feel that badly on her behalf, but on the other hand, she's pregnant, and if you kill him, his child will grow up without a father. But again on the third hand, he's probably the least fuckable, if you're being honest, he has let himself go recently, and there is nothing about him that's particularly fuckworthy.

The old friend is unmarried but has a lover who he has been with for many years, and they have no children or interest in having children. You aren't close anymore because you and the old friend had a falling out, and while it was many years ago, you still harbor some resentment. You could kill the old friend as revenge, but then, you would stand out immediately as a suspect, and also, you've spent all these years being the bigger person, not seeking revenge when you could have, being generous whenever possible. After all this time invested in one-upping the old friend, being a better old friend, you don't want to ruin that by murdering the old friend, because you feel certain that once you have murdered the old friend you are no longer the better friend.

You decide that maybe it would help if you paid the three potential candidates a visit, to see if maybe you feel differently about them after seeing them and assessing their value as people on a face-to-face basis. After discussing this with your boyfriend, he agrees that this isn't a violation of the rules as long as someone gets fucked and killed and fucked. After all, he says, we are just making things up as we go along.

You meet the business contact for coffee, which is something you had been talking about doing for ages anyway. You sit across a small round table from him and you both drink from oversized mugs of very elaborate flavored coffee. Yours has both caramel and vanilla; it is very rich. His has hickory and something else, you don't remember what exactly. You think hickory in coffee is an abomination. The business contact talks a little bit about the business things you both do, and it is very business-y, and you half pay attention while you decide whether you want to have sex with him or kill him. You only have to kill one person, and you are still considering saving one of your fucks for the casual acquaintance, in order to spare his child the pain of being half-orphaned before it's even born.

The business contact is more handsome than you'd imagined he'd be. He is appetizingly athletic, he has a friendly, open face and prominent eyebrows, and when he smiles, his eyes light up in a very attractive fashion. It seems like it would be silly not to fuck this person, and then he compliments you on your handling of a business matter you were both involved in several months ago, and you decide that you're going to go ahead and fuck him.

You fuck the business contact, and afterward he is sitting in bed with his iPad, answering emails, and then he takes a Skype call, and you are on your phone the whole time playing a game about cats. You like the cat game. The business contact expects you to leave, and you expect you to leave, but then you start to feel a little twinge of regret, just a twinge, like maybe you had too much fun with the business contact, you liked him a little too much, and now that you have fucked him there is a lingering concern that you are now connected to the business contact, and maybe you always will be, a door open, because you have shared a physical intimacy and also because while you are playing your phone game about cats, you think of the business contact's smile, his mastery at the business which you are both involved in, and his friendly enthusiasm as a lover.

So when he hangs up his Skype call and looks at you expectantly, you kill him. You kill him extra hard, just to be sure, beat him with the big wooden lamp and then with the metal sculpture of an elephant he keeps on the night stand, and then just to be just super certain about it, you go in the kitchen and get a knife and you knife him a few times. Then you take a shower and get dressed and pour bleach generously over absolutely everything you think you might have touched, hoping that will be enough to take care of fingerprints and DNA.

On your way out, you look at the business contact, a kind of wet, mushy dead on the bed, now reeking of bleach, and you feel hollow and needy and a particular kind of empty, and you feel fairly certain you did the right thing there.

So you go to meet the casual acquaintance next, thinking this will be easy, you just fuck him and then fuck your old friend, which will be unpleasant, and then it's over, but you wind up killing the casual acquaintance too. That winds up also being an impulse thing because when you see him he's a little drunk and sloppy and falling over, and he's really let himself go, you can't stress enough how much he's let himself go, like he's lumpy-looking but also it seems like he's given up on washing his face or brushing his teeth or applying moisturizer anywhere. You're a bad person, you think as you're killing him, because really being generally unhygienic is not a good reason to kill someone but your instincts assure you that this was the right thing to do. You back your car over the casual acquaintance a few times for good measure. It's raining while you do it. Killing people is a very wet business, you're discovering.

You think about going to meet the old friend, but you're overwhelmed by how uncomfortable that will wind up being, and you realize that you'd very much rather not do that. It will be hard to fuck the friend without meeting him. You consider a disguise, like maybe a wig and a big hat and a too-large coat to disguise yourself. So you've got your wig and your big hat and your too-large coat, and you add some sunglasses, and then you walk with a limp, because that seems distinctively not you, because you don't have a limp.

You're on your way with your bulky disguise and your limp and then at the last minute you buy a greeting card that says SORRY with a picture of a puppy making a mess on the front, and you apply a pretty liberal dosage of anthrax to the envelope, and instead of going to go meet your old friend, you go to the post office and mail the anthrax and you think, having mustered several years of forgiveness and goodwill, you're still the better person on the aggregate even if you did wind up taking revenge.

You report all this to your boyfriend. I lost the game, you say mournfully. Neither of you have ever lost a game before, but ultimately you only fucked one person and killed three of them, and no matter how generously you read the rules, you are not victorious. Your boyfriend has been out too, fucking and killing people, but he followed the rules of the game and you declare him the winner. You take a shower together and you kiss and have a little sex, and then you both pack bags with some clothes and beloved possessions, because after all you've both killed a few people at this point, and when you started the game you didn't think about how easy it is to get caught for this sort of thing, in this day and age.

Later, you are both in the car that you bought off Craigslist for a few hundred dollars. It's a manual transmission, but when your hand is free between gear shifts, you hold your boyfriend's hand. You play other games, you play I spy, you play the license plate game, you play I'm Going on a Picnic. It's only after about six hundred miles that your boyfriend says, Fuck, Marry, Kill.

Yes, you say.

VII

Boyfriends All the Way Down

Universal Boyfriend Theory

AT THE CENTER of the universe, the boyfriend singularity pops out boyfriends at a rate of approximately one per hour, forever. The boyfriend singularity can create a variety of different boyfriends depending on the arrangement and intensity of the heavy elements and gasses spinning at its heart at any given moment. So the boyfriend singularity creates tall boyfriends, short boyfriends, thin boyfriends, fat boyfriends, very fat boyfriends, pale boyfriends and brown boyfriends and black boyfriends, rich boyfriends and poor boyfriends, kind, intimate boyfriends and distant, withholding boyfriends, polite boyfriends and rude boyfriends, deferential boyfriends and braggadocious boyfriends, the gentlest and cruelest boyfriends, boyfriends made of stone, boyfriends made of strong organic fibers, boyfriends made of millions of tiny flowers delicately laced together, boyfriends made of concrete, boyfriends made of steel, boyfriends made of glass, white-hot boyfriends burning like stars. Every kind of boyfriend is born at the heart of the boyfriend singularity, and each one is the best boyfriend, even the hurtful ones, the cruel-tongued ones, the ones who disappear before you even really know them. Every boyfriend that emerges from the boyfriend singularity is the best boyfriend that has ever emerged from the boyfriend singularity, and it continues on in this way, boyfriends all the way down.

From your spaceship, you watch the boyfriends emerge from the boyfriend singularity. You take measurements and readings. You have a long table of boyfriend instruments taking readings, constant boyfriend calculations. The process is so automated that you have to do almost nothing except watch through the wide, thick window as each boyfriend materializes from the singularity. All you can do is wait for enough data. You hope to one day be able to predict what kind of boyfriend will come out of the boyfriend singularity. But you are not close to that breakthrough, or you don't think you are. It was a victory just to perfect the instrument that tells you whether the boyfriends are nice or mean.

Often when the boyfriends are born, they immediately leave the vicinity of the boyfriend singularity, flying off to a particular corner of the universe at incredible speed. But some of them stay, living on the asteroids that circle the singularity, tiny satellites. These are the boyfriends that cannot go to live on any planet, boyfriends made of toxic gasses or heavy metals or dangerous elements, boyfriends whose bodies burn so brightly no planet could survive their proximity, or give off radiation so strong that the instruments in front of you pulse with red caution; don't go near, they say. Eventually you would like to collect a sample, study a boyfriend more closely, but not these boyfriends. You have been in space a long time, long enough that you are not afraid of much, but you still fear death. That is the human center of you.

When you went to Space School, they told you space was not black but grey, the colors so muted and subtle that the human eye cannot quite perceive them. Every picture you've seen of space is a lie, your Space Instructor explained, colored by artists to seem more beautiful and dynamic to the human eye. Real space will appear flat and grey to your eyes, he said. The example he used was that your eye is like a camera made of meat. A camera made of meat would not be a very good camera, he said by way of explanation, and in the years that followed, you often imagined going to the deli and picking up several pounds of thinly-sliced turkey and chicken and ham in order to make a meat-camera that was also an eye, the eye of some meat-being that was also you and everyone you know.

You went into space prepared for unending monotony, and there is a lot of that, but the truth is that your Space Instructor knew almost nothing about space and warned you about all of the wrong things. You and your crewmates have been out here for almost two hundred years, and you've seen that real space is not one color but many. In this part of space, the part of space where the boyfriends are born, space is white, a muted beige-white like apartment walls. In many ways this color is even more disturbing than the strange dark grey that space was before, even more disturbing than the parts of space that were pitch-black, where you couldn't see meteors until they struck you. It is so white you have to wear special modified sunglasses to protect your eyes, your meat-cameras; it is so white that you feel like you are always about to run into the white walls of your apartment, or worse, so white that you will never run into anything, ever.

The boyfriend singularity is unlike anything you've ever seen in any part of space. The bright, violent color of the boyfriend singularity is what caused your navigator to stop in the first place. The boyfriend singularity spread across the whiteness of space, all hot pink and purple, fleshy. You joked with the navigator that it looks like someone's butt just after you spank it too hard. It's a weak joke, because it really does look like that, but the navigator wasn't listening; he was watching two boyfriends play hopscotch on a large, flat hunk of space rock. You were both quiet for a while before you decided that this anomaly warranted further study.

There are four people on your spaceship. There is you, and you are the scientist. It is your job to conduct studies, collect and analyze samples, conduct research. In practice, you are more like a librarian, keeping track of specimens, making sure everything is clearly labeled, answering questions, looking things up on the ship's computer. You have brought along several specimens, different kinds of plant and animal life, and in that way, you are also like a zookeeper, except sometimes you have to test the plants and animals to see how being in space has impacted them. Although you are not really a doctor, you also occasionally run tests on your fellow crewmembers, checking blood oxygenation and bone density, reading aloud a questionnaire to check for depression. You have huge boxes full of pills to give them for almost any ailment. You also have a small list of ailments which, if diagnosed in a crewmember, would necessitate that crewmember being released out of an airlock.

Along with you, there is the navigator, who is supposed to pilot the ship. However, space is so large, and so little of it is charted that in practice the navigator's job is just to stop if he sees anything interesting. Along with you and the navigator, there is a soldier, whose job is to protect the crew of the spaceship, you guess from space pirates or hostile aliens or something along those lines. So far, he hasn't done much except push-ups. There is also a poet, who came along so that someone could talk about how beautiful space is, but the poet is useless for that. Mostly, he writes poems about having sex with women and how much he misses smelling flowers, and gravity. Sometimes he gives readings of his poems, after which the soldier says, That had nothing to do with space.

The day you discovered the boyfriend singularity, the poet was the first to run up to see why you'd stopped. He, too, stared at the boyfriends, wondering at their existence. Doesn't it look like a butt just after you've spanked it too hard? You ask the poet, hoping he will understand your use of metaphor, but he just shrugs a little shrug.

It was a good joke, you mutter under your breath, and after that you vow to spank the poet's butt too hard later, just so you can show everyone that it is exactly what the boyfriend singularity looks like. You have been in space for two hundred years, and your sexual mores have devolved over time. Sex has become a way of putting off the mind-numbing monotony of only knowing four people, and in this way it is not so different from your life on Earth. You were also sent various other kinds of entertainment, off-brand imitations of Tetris, and, because someone had a sense of humor, Space Invaders, as well as a database of books and movies and TV shows and music. Still, it turns out that two hundred years is enough time to consume all of the relevant parts of your culture.

You and the poet were lovers and then ex-lovers before you went into space; in fact, it was you who recommended the poet for the job, although you didn't think much of his writing, even then. In space, once you had both watched every movie and TV show you had always wanted to get caught up on, you resumed being lovers, and then the poet and the soldier became lovers, and then you and the navigator, and then the navigator and the soldier, then the soldier and you, then the poet and the navigator, and it went on like that until you were all lovers, an indistinct mush of attachment. You pushed all of your beds together and slept nestled in each other like a row of spoons, or sometimes more chaotically, a pile of branches, limbs sticking out at strange angles. Really, the four of you are trying to become Russian dolls, swallow each other and become one, but even in space there is physics to contend with.

The heart of the matter is that this is the reason you stopped to study the boyfriends. The boyfriends, with their near-infinite variety, are, perhaps, the least boring thing in the universe. You, and the rest of the crew, are afraid if you start the engines up again, leave the boyfriend singularity behind you, you will be leaving behind the only interesting thing you will ever see for the rest of your lives, which will be long, excruciatingly long, and you will be left with just each other. So although you now know that the boyfriend singularity will continue to create one boyfriend per hour, forever, you keep hoping that your instruments will reveal something more about them, something that would require further research, further study, more time spent at the edge of the boyfriend singularity, which, after you spend an hour with the poet, the whole crew comes to agree definitely looks exactly like a butt just after you've spanked it too hard, even though they still don't think that is a particularly funny thing to say.

You are fine-tuning the instrument that tells you about each boyfriend's preferences with regard to musical theater, postmodern literature, and adult films, as well as whether they are a cat person or a dog person, when the soldier comes to your laboratory. It's not exactly big enough for two people, but if you slide over on your bench, you can make room for the soldier to sit down and enjoy a decent view of the boyfriend singularity through the window, and it's only a little bit cramped for both of you. After all the years you've spent in space, the soldier is the only one who still wears his uniform. It is pressed, neatly tucked in, and still has two gold bars at the collar and chevrons pinned to the cuffs. His hair, too, is regulation, cropped close to his head, his beard short and neatly-trimmed. The beard is not exactly regulation but it is the one concession the soldier makes to the fact that he will probably never see a senior officer in person again for the rest of his life, even though none of you knows exactly how long that might be. The poet likes to conjecture that since you will all live forever, it is possible that you will see all things, possible and impossible, before the universe again recedes to a single white-hot point of fire and everything vanishes. He offered this as an explanation for the boyfriend singularity before he scratched his hip and went back to his room to sleep. The poet keeps odd hours. The navigator protested that this was awful science, not really science at all, but the poet didn't really care.

The universe is not now, nor will it ever be, a single white-hot point of fire, the navigator said. Privately, you weren't so sure, but you were sure the poet doesn't know anything worth knowing about space.

Despite occasionally being lovers, you and the soldier have always had the most difficult relationship. The soldier even gets along better with the poet than with you, so it is strange that he would come to where you work and sit so close to you and you think perhaps he wants or needs something. For example, the soldier has infrequent herpes outbreaks. He had it before you came to space, so now you all have it, although the soldier is the only one who ever manifests symptoms, except, once, the poet. Sometimes he comes to you for a course of Valtrex, which is a pill that you have in abundance in one of your large bins full of pills, and you wonder if he was tested for it and they knew he had it before you all went to space together, or whether it just never came up and you were provided with a stockpile of Valtrex since statistically, one of you would probably need it at some point. Or it could have been provided as insurance against some other eventuality you haven't encountered yet.

Instead, the soldier says, Have you considered trying to take a sample?

You ask if by take a sample he means just kidnapping one of the boyfriends from space.

It wouldn't work, you say and you gesture to one of the boyfriends doing push-ups on a passing asteroid, his skin glowing a wicked red, his body limned in blue fire, they're too dangerous to have on board the ship.

One of the normal ones, the soldier said, that flies past the ship occasionally. It's true the navigator has had to quickly move the ship out of the trajectory of several boyfriends flying off toward some distant planet, to live there and be a boyfriend on whatever planet has boyfriends. Most of them are flying so fast when they leave the gravity of the boyfriend singularity that they would blow through the ship like a missile.

At that moment, you and the soldier watch as the boyfriend singularity births a boyfriend that looks like a dinosaur, large and covered in scales and feathers. Instead of arms it has wide, feathered wings, in iridescent green and blue. When the boyfriend singularity creates a boyfriend, it flashes slightly, its colors becoming even more intense, and then the boyfriend walks out of the center like he is walking through a door. After he has fully emerged, he looks around, stretches, yawns, and flies away. This is what the dinosaur boyfriend does. He smiles what you assume to be a dinosaur smile before he vanishes, plunging straight down into the egg-colored space that surrounds you all in every direction.

The soldier turns to you and begins to rub your shoulders. Because this is a cramped space, he has to contort to do it, leaning both back and sideways and turning sharply at the waist in a way that you imagine must not be comfortable for him in the slightest. It is not comfortable for you either. The soldier has broad, short-fingered hands and has clearly not given many shoulder rubs. He is perhaps not the worst shoulder-rubber on the ship—that prize goes to the poet, so utterly lacking in empathy and exterior focus that his understanding of what another person might find pleasurable was, at best, limited—but he is not as good as, say, the navigator, who is both thoughtful and affectionate. Mostly it is just the gesture itself, so unlike the soldier, that you think he is perhaps trying to butter you up, to bribe you into something but you're not sure what. Capturing one of the boyfriends, you suppose, and as you think about it you think about some kind of energy net, or a magnetic array that might draw the boyfriend off-course. The soldier has leaned close to you, is breathing on your ear and neck with his wet breath, but you are far off inside your head, doing the math you know how to do, doing the thing you do best, which is figuring things out. You are imagining ways you might catch a boyfriend flying through space.

Another way, you think, that might work is simply choosing a boyfriend and following it with the ship, moving as fast as the engines will carry you, in order to keep up, to find the place that the boyfriends know how to find. Although before you had assumed that they were all going to different places, the opposite could also be true. The configuration of space is such that each boyfriend could actually be going to the same place, but arriving by different routes. You try to imagine what advantages such circuitous approaches might confer when you realize that the soldier has placed his hand somewhere near the small of your back, and you shelve thoughts of the boyfriends for now in order to turn your attention to rebuffing the soldier, with whom you would prefer not to have intercourse at exactly this moment. Even after all the time you've spent together you and the soldier have never seemed to be exactly sexually compatible, or perhaps you are so thoroughly sexually compatible it is impossible for you to have sex with each other. It is usually more like a fight, you and the soldier, because you are both striving for dominance and control, and it's a pretty well-known fact that two people cannot have dominance and control at the same time. You are not a sociologist or a psychologist but this seems manifestly true to you.

You try to turn away from the soldier, who tries to hold you where you sit. You twist your body and he twists and tightens his hands, and for a moment there is a struggle, confined to the tiny amount of cabin space in your lab. The soldier growls a little in the back of his throat and you turn your face towards his. He thinks that he has succeeded in luring you into a sexual encounter, but instead you pull your head back a bit and then slam the bridge of his nose with your forehead, hard. His arms, which had almost entirely encircled your waist, loosen almost immediately as he draws back. You see that his nose is broken, blood already mixing with the brown, red, and white hairs of his beard. Your forehead hurts quite a bit. For the soldier, the mood has been killed, and he pouts like a child, cupping his nose gently with both hands, though whether to protect it or catch the falling blood, you aren't sure.

You place your hand gently on the soldier's bicep and ask him if he would like something for his nose, for the pain. You pull a first aid kit off the wall and begin to sponge up the blood, pulling his hands gently to his lap, where they sit limply. I'm sorry, this is going to hurt, you say, and you set the soldier's nose so it won't heal crooked. Later, both of his eyes will be black and blue. You give him a mild painkiller; you ask if he's been taking his medication. He says that he has and, looking at his face, you believe him. Dry

swallowing his pills, the soldier leaves, still pouting, carrying a wounded air. You would expect him to be tougher,
but he's not. None of you really are, not anymore. You are
sensitive and childish. You are horny and violent and barely
under control.

When the process of long-term deep space exploration
was first studied on your home planet, the main concern
was that there was no engine able to fly through space fast
enough for a human to survive the trip. Getting anywhere
at all cost an entire human lifetime, getting to multiple
places cost multiple lifetimes, and so on. Engine speeds
improved, with subsequent missions reaching further and
further, but the ceiling on interstellar travel was reached
and the amount of space reachable by a human being in
their life was still pitifully small compared to the size and
breadth of the universe. Scientists began to explore other
options. Studies were conducted on the idea of multiple
generations of explorers, pregnant women in space giving
birth to future generations of explorers. There were, of
course, problems with this, including the fact that inbreed-
ing would become an almost immediate problem. But, further to that, when trials were conducted, it was discovered
that babies born in space were generally not viable. Something always went wrong, they were born without brains
or with bones like jelly, or with no faces, just blank skin
stretched across their skulls. The babies born in space got
progressively weirder and weirder, babies tentacled, babies
with hundreds of extra ears, babies born covered in tumors.
The scientists ultimately decided that this would not be the
solution to their conundrum.

There were other experiments. Hypersleep and time compression and cellular regeneration chambers. All of them proved to have undesirable side effects. It took decades for them to invent you, and the soldier, and the poet, and the navigator: ordinary humans made immortal for the purposes of studying every square inch of space over their infinite lifetimes. You don't know how they did it. You were born mortal, to an ordinary family who lived in an ordinary city in the middle of nowhere, and you got good grades in school and eventually you got a PhD and you joined the space program. You were in excellent shape but no more immortal than anyone else, you thought.

You went to sleep, they put you under, and when you woke up they told you that you would explore space for millions of years and you would never die. You didn't believe them except after that you never got older. You went to space school, you went to flight school, you studied extensively all of the science you would need to survive in space, and then you went into space, first for a hundred years, then for two hundred, and you never aged a day through all of that.

You don't know how they did it, but here you are. While you, and the navigator, and the poet, and the soldier, suffer what you suspect are a variety of increasingly devastating mental breakdowns, your bodies remain young and healthy. Your bodies will, you suspect, outlive your minds.

The navigator has given the poet a haircut, you discover when you leave your lab for the day. Obviously, you don't really have a day, there is no sun that rises and sets in space to mark the passage of time. But you all observe very strict schedules. You have set your clocks to Central Time, Central Earth Time, so on your ship it is always roughly the same time it would be in Chicago, or Minneapolis, or Houston. In order to preserve a sense of normalcy, you go to work in the morning and you leave work in the late afternoon and go to bed at a reasonable hour.

You find the poet and the navigator in the common area of the ship, the poet seated in one of the dining chairs and the navigator, with a pair of clippers, cleaning up the back of the poet's head. All around their feet are piles of the poet's hair, thick dark curls scattered across the clean floor. The poet has had his hair almost shaved, with just a few millimeters of hair left at the top. You can see his brown scalp through the tiny hairs. When the navigator finishes his work, you rub your hands all over the poet's head, feeling his bristly hair against your palms. You rub the back of his head and then move your hand down to cup the back of his neck in the way that you know he likes. You are hoping to lure him into a sexual encounter, but then you see the soldier, sitting alone at the table, his face bruised, glowering, and you touch the poet with less urgency.

The navigator asks about the soldier and you explain what happened in the lab. The navigator frowns sympathetically, touches your shoulder gently and asks if you are alright. Really your head hurts, but you tell the navigator you're fine. He asks the soldier if he is doing ok, rubs his shoulders and whispers something in his ear, probably some comfort. You ask the soldier if he needs anything, a painkiller maybe. Or a mood stabilizer. The soldier waves you off gruffly. He is trying to be tough in front of the navigator and the poet. Your life on the ship includes periodic moments of schoolyard discomfort.

Outside, the boyfriend singularity flushes scarlet, but none of you are around to see it. The navigator is playing a game of cards with the poet. The soldier is reading a detective novel, an actual paperback, yellowed and worn at the edges. It is one of the handful of personal items you know that he brought with him, although you don't know why. You asked him once why that book was so important when you probably had an electronic copy on the ship's many databases, but if he even knows what moved him to do that, he certainly did not share that with you. You know the soldier loves to read, though. He does it more than any of the rest of you, even the poet, who hardly reads at all. You are sitting at the end of the table watching the poet and the navigator play their card game. Earlier you made a game of trying to help one or the other of them cheat, but like many things you do, it seemed to be the wrong impulse at the wrong time. Nobody wanted to play your game.

The boyfriend created by the boyfriend singularity strikes your ship at incredible speed, immediately piercing the hull. The whole ship rocks off its orbit for a moment, but it's enough of a lurch to send all of you flying across the room. Later, you are relieved and surprised that injuries to your crewmates were not more serious. The soldier broke a rib, and the navigator might have a concussion. You put yourself between the poet and the wall, so while he is uninjured, you have an impressive bruise across your torso. You check yourself over and it seems like nothing is too badly injured. The navigator offers to perform the rudimentary first aid that he knows, but you turn him down.

After you've all collected yourselves, you begin a check of the ship. The navigator goes to the cockpit to work on re-establishing stable orbit, while you go down to your workstation to check on life support and make sure the gravity still works. There is no engineer, and you don't know what exactly you would do if the ship had sustained greater damage than your limited abilities could repair. The navigator, who possesses the greatest technical knowledge among the four of you, would not be able to repair, say, the engine, if it were to suddenly cease function. It was built by a room full of genius scientists, none of whom was interested in coming along on the mission once their project was completed.

The soldier and the poet find the boyfriend lodged in a kind of cocoon of metal made of the remains of the hull where he penetrated it. He fortunately landed in a cargo bay that is not often used. It was expected that you would be doing a lot of on loading and offloading, but it seems the opposite is the case. None of you have ever so much as been down there, much less used it for its intended purpose. Where would you be taking cargo from? Or sending it to? Miraculously, the boyfriend is alive and seems unhurt. The soldier says this over the ship's radio and you don't believe him. You ask the soldier to bring the boyfriend to the medical bay, so you can look him over. It's possible he was very badly injured in the collision, you say, please try not to jostle him too much or it could do permanent damage. The soldier resents taking your orders, but he does. He tells you that he and the poet are on their way with the boyfriend.

The boyfriend is unimaginably beautiful, so much so that you feel an irrational possessive claim to him immediately. He is a strange composite of the four of you. He has the poet's curly, tousled dark hair, the soldier's square jaw, the navigator's clear brown skin. You think maybe the boyfriend singularity missed you because he doesn't have any of your features, but then he opens his eyes and he has your eyes, striking and greenish-gold. When he sits up, your boyfriend looks sure and calm, like he is exactly where he is supposed to be. He extends his hand and shakes yours, then the soldier's, then the poet's. He beams at all of you, and when he turns his smile on the soldier, you feel a surge of possessive anger. You don't want the boyfriend to belong to the soldier, who you are convinced would treat him with insufficient care. You meet the soldier's eyes and he is looking back at you, glaring with his cruel face.

Hello, you say. Do you know where you came from?

The boyfriend points vaguely in the direction of outside, space, the anomaly. It's a careless gesture; his eyes, so much like your own, say clearly that he knows exactly where he came from and you know it too. The soldier widens his stance and crosses his arms over his chest. The poet, too, looks jealous, standing taller and squaring his shoulders. The tension that falls over all of you is palpable. Your boyfriend smiles charmingly. He hums a little song. You wonder how the boyfriend singularity created him, how it was able to aggregate the four of you together in that way. You wonder if, while you observed the singularity, the singularity perhaps observed you in return. It knew your schedule; the boyfriend came while you were all off-duty, unprepared. The boyfriends had previously emerged at very regular intervals, namely, one per hour, forever, or so you thought. You could track and predict each next boyfriend's emergence with ease. That is how the navigator had managed to avoid being struck, until now. The idea that the boyfriend singularity contains some heretofore unknown intelligence fills you with dread, a dread that intrudes on your other, less complicated feelings, desire and jealousy and anger.

You are angry at the soldier. It seems like he is always in the way. He is always encroaching on the things you have, like he would like to steal them. He stole the poet from you, you see now, and you didn't mind at the time because you all had each other and you could share freely because you were all trapped together, the four of you, for all time. Even now the poet has taken the soldier's side, stands beside him, while he should have been beside you. But that feeling, that perhaps everyone belongs to everyone, does not exist with your boyfriend. Your boyfriend is rare and special and clearly was meant to belong to one of you. He was clearly meant to belong to you. You do not see how you could share your boyfriend, even with the navigator, who you greatly like and respect. You like and respect the navigator less as you begin to imagine him sexually with your boyfriend.

Without realizing it, you have begun to run your fingers through your boyfriend's hair. It's perfect, perfectly soft. It is exactly like the poet's hair, which you loved, before he cut it off. In your imagination you have built a life with your boyfriend. You imagine having a small house with him, the kind of house a new couple gets, where you and he would live and garden and pursue various hobbies. You think you would like to paint; your boyfriend would write. You would have a studio in the garage where sometimes he would bring you a cup of hot tea or a glass of lemonade. On cold days, he would insist you wear a sweater. Sometimes you would go into his office and drag him away from the computer to make love. In your version of your future with your boyfriend, you and he make love vigorously, and often. You get a dog, an English bulldog with a flat, wrinkled face, ugly but good-natured.

In your imaginary life, you and your boyfriend can't agree what kind of sofa to get for your new home. Your old one needs replacing. Before you, it belonged to an old lady who had wrapped it in plastic for forty years. You bought it for a few dollars on Craigslist after she died. Your boyfriend hates the couch and you have to admit that you aren't in love with it, it was just a cheap thing that someone else agreed to deliver. But now you are making a life with your boyfriend. He smiles at you warmly as you walk in the furniture store. In your imaginary version of your life with your boyfriend, you both sit on various couches and imagine your lives with the new couch. Your boyfriend would like to get something tall enough that the dog can't climb on it. You would like to get something large enough that the two of you could nap on it together, your boyfriend nestled into your body. You say you would be like two spoons, and your boyfriend agrees with you. He always agrees with you. In your imaginary version of your life with your boyfriend, you never fight or disagree. You never go to bed angry or feel angry at all. He loves everything you do, and he never does anything that would make you upset. It is the perfect life.

You don't consider that, in the middle of space, in your spaceship, it is unlikely that you will ever return home to Earth. Nobody even knows which way it is. The navigator has some chance of finding a way back, maybe, but it would take hundreds of years, and anything could have happened on Earth and anything could happen to you on your way to Earth. You are in a part of space that is not just uncharted but has not even been theorized, and you are alone there, you and the soldier and the navigator and the poet and, most importantly, your boyfriend.

We should take him to the crew quarters and let him get some sleep, you say.

He doesn't look tired, the poet says.

Why do you get to decide what we do? the soldier says.

Fine, you were prepared for the possibility of an altercation with the soldier. In fact, it was inevitable. The soldier is a bully and you are a hero, and it is the job of heroes to stop bullies from being bullies. You have a strong sense of right and wrong.

I'm in charge, you say.

Says who, the soldier says, you're not the captain.

It's true, you aren't the captain. There isn't a captain on the ship. It was assumed you would all interact with each other symbiotically and that you would arrive at decisions as a group. You were all selected because your personality profiles integrated in such a way that you would get along. The navigator is extremely reasonable, the soldier is decisive, you are intelligent, the poet is passive. Decisions were to be reached by consensus, and anyway, there are no decisions. The navigator decides where to go; you decide what to study; the soldier decides when there is danger; the poet makes unknowable aesthetic decisions.

I'm in charge of studying the singularity, you say, and he is part of the singularity. I'm in charge of studying him.

The soldier bristles, stands up tall, clenches his fist. You aren't the captain, he repeats.

What's going on, the navigator, who has returned from the cockpit, interrupts.

I'm just trying to bring him to the crew quarters, where he can rest, you say.

He's not going anywhere, the soldier says.

What do you intend to do with him here, the navigator asks.

The soldier has no answer. The poet pipes in to argue that there should be some discussion of the stranger on your ship and what should be done with him. The navigator agrees, but also says, in the meantime, you should walk your boyfriend back to the crew quarters.

When you take your boyfriend to the crew quarters, he smiles at you. It's the same smile you remember from before, from your life together. Before you know it, you're dragging the boyfriend by the arm, headed for an escape pod. You have no plan, other than the possibility of pointing the escape pod in the direction of Earth, and your future life together. It won't be easy; the escape pod has little food and few supplies for the journey back to Earth, but you think there must be another planet closer. You don't need food or supplies anyway, or at least you don't think. You think you're immortal. You think that the boyfriend can survive long journeys through space. You want your life with your boyfriend anywhere. There are other planets that have little houses on pretty streets where two people who are in love can live together. After all, there's no evidence your boyfriend was even supposed to come to your ship. He could have been headed anywhere, to another planet that happened to be in your same direction. It would be difficult but you could find a place for you and your boyfriend to be together.

When you get to the escape pods, though, you find that they're all gone and the soldier is waiting for you with one of his long-bladed knives. He used to collect them, on earth. You have admired this particular knife before. With one arm, you push the boyfriend behind you, although you know what the soldier wants and that he won't put the boyfriend in danger. Instead, you and the soldier have an altercation. You narrowly avoid getting stabbed, but you're also unsuccessful in blowing the soldier out of an airlock. He's thought of that. The controls are all jammed. Instead, in the scuffle, you trip him, and as he falls backwards you break away and run as fast as you can, your boyfriend in tow.

You make your way back to the common area, grabbing a large wrench from a repair kit along the way. The soldier, who is bigger and slower than you, arrives a moment later, and the navigator and the poet rush in from the other direction.

Let's just calm down, the navigator says.

I am very calm, you say.

The soldier, who is not calm, rushes you again with the large knife. Maybe it's more of a machete. You fight him with the wrench, which is almost the size of your arm. Though you manage to hold your own, you feel like the soldier will overwhelm you soon. You are not a soldier, have never really had the stomach for combat. But you see, out of the corner of your eye, your boyfriend standing beside the navigator, his brow furrowed, a sad look on his face. Your heart breaks for him, and with renewed strength, you manage to break the soldier's arm.

He clutches it, growling and glaring at you. You can see a glint in his eye that tells you he is imagining his life with the boyfriend too, maybe in the very same house on the very same street. You set your jaw. You can't let that happen. You grip the wrench with both hands, thinking you might kill the soldier, a quick blow to the head, when the soldier pulls an energy weapon with his off hand. He must have had it on his person somewhere. Immediately, you think that he's gone crazy. Only a crazy person would fire an energy weapon in here. You aren't even sure if they work. They were inconsistent in testing and they gave you two of them, for emergencies or threats that defied conventional means. You don't even know how the soldier got one out of its case; it should require two keys to open.

Okay, the navigator says, holding his hand out, in a placating manner. Okay. Let's be rational about this. Only a crazy person would fire one of those things in here. If you hit a wall, the cabin depressurizes, and probably we will all die.

The poet is crying. Please, he says, please. You can't take your eyes off of the poet, or your hand off of your boyfriend behind you.

The soldier holds the gun steady. Likely, he does not intend to miss, and you don't think he'll miss either. The navigator is still speaking in a low, calm voice, trying to convince the soldier to stand down. The poet is still crying, big heartbreaking sobs. Otherwise, the room is still and quiet, until suddenly you feel your boyfriend's hand on your back. You think he intends to push you out of the way.

After that, three unrelated things happen at once: you turn to grab your boyfriend, the soldier fires his weapon, and the entire ship lurches violently. One of the stabilizers, which had been damaged with the boyfriend's impact, fails, and as a result the entire ship is suddenly on its side. You manage to put yourself between your boyfriend and the wall, and as a result, you crack your head on the metal of the hull and lose consciousness for a few minutes.

When you come to, everything is quiet. You check first for the boyfriend, who is alive, but has some bad bruises. The soldier is just returning to consciousness, and the navigator is hunched over the poet, who, you can see, has died. The soldier's shot went wild when the ship rolled; the poet was in the way. You kneel, next to the navigator, over the poet. His chest and stomach are covered in blood. Without thinking, your hand goes to his head. You run your palm over his recently buzzed head, feeling the bristly hairs on your fingers. You vow never to forget the feeling.

The soldier is standing over you; he's sniffling like a child on the verge of tears. He keeps saying that he's sorry, that he just loves you so much, and he couldn't bear to lose you that way. He just wanted to keep you. He didn't want anyone else to have you.

You are thinking of the poet and it takes you a moment to realize that you're crying, in fact, howling. Your whole body heaves. The poet was awful and you realize suddenly that you loved him so much, right to your core. You are awful too. You and the poet were meant to be awful together.

Weeping over the poet's dead body, you imagine a world where you and the poet never left earth. You lived in an apartment together, you both taught at a local college. You would have two cats. One is Sandy, the other is Olivia. They're both named after Olivia Newton-John, in a way.

You didn't have much, and you fought all the time. You would fight over everything. Your house is too small. You would fight and then you would make love, or sometimes you would just fuck. Sometimes you are so frustrated with the poet that you just hatefuck him, right there on the old lady's couch you bought for a few bucks off Craigslist from her grieving son. Sometimes he's so frustrated with you that he tries to hatefuck you back. But to you he is everything, everywhere. When you imagine life with the poet, he is the whole world, and he is also something very small that lives inside your body. Sometimes when you look at him, when you imagine a different you looking at him, the whole world changes and then you change. You would live the worst life with the poet, in sad jobs you hate, drinking beer by a lake. It feels like it should be awful, but as you watch the whole scenario spin out before your eyes, it seems like you've never felt better in your life.

VIII

You Are Waiting
for a Foundation to Crack

The Village with All of the Boyfriends

THE VILLAGE WITH All of the Boyfriends is where all of your boyfriends wind up eventually. You built this Village for them and they can't leave and neither can you. You are not allowed inside, but you wait in the desert at the edge of town, you pace, sometimes you stomp a sleeping leg until it wakes up, sometimes you sit cross-legged in the dust. You spit and the ground soaks it up.

You try not to watch the boyfriends but you watch them.

The boyfriends ride motorcycles. They go to the beach and eat hot dogs with mustard and drink diet soda. The boyfriends learn to solve mysteries from TV. Some of them write poems and some of them post their political writings on blogs. They laugh easily. They get drunk and kiss. They go to the gym, spin class, yoga, water aerobics, ballet. They write long letters to their mothers, who like you even less now.

The Village is overflowing with boyfriends. There are boyfriends on every street, in every house, boyfriends crowding the General Store and gossiping in line at the Bank and behind the counter at the Laundromat. Boyfriends serve meals to other boyfriends packed into tiny booths at the Taqueria.

Boyfriends sleep two and three to a bed, dozens on the floors, on the kitchen table, on the couch, on the bathroom counter, squeezed into the tub. Every day it seems like there's a new boyfriend and he has to sleep on a windowsill or in an empty hutch.

Boyfriends perch on the power lines and boyfriends sit on every inch of every rooftop. On a nice day, their blonde hair catches the sunlight and it looks like every roof is shingled with gold. On rainy days, their hair darkens and their white shirts cling to their backs and chests.

The roofs have begun to sag with the weight of the boyfriends, the support beams crack, wood floors have started to buckle. The damage caused by the boyfriends is structural. The buildings slump to the ground. Everywhere the boyfriends are too much weight pressing down on the houses, the General Store, the Bank, the Laundromat, the Taqueria. Out on the edge of town you are bow-legged with the strain of it.

You are waiting for a foundation to crack.

Biographical note

Zachary Doss was a writer and editor whose work appeared in *Sonora Review*, *Fourteen Hills*, *Fairy Tale Review*, *Caketrain*, *DIAGRAM*, *Paper Darts*, and other journals. His short story "Bespoke" was the winner of the 2016 Puerto del Sol Short Fiction Contest. He held an MFA in creative writing from the University of Alabama, where he taught composition and rhetoric, literature, and creative writing. He was also pursuing a PhD in creative writing and literature at the University of Southern California at the time of his death.

Note

On behalf of Zachary Doss, we would like to express our gratitude:

To the magazines and editors who published his writing.

To the AWP Award Series and Kelly Link for selecting *Boy Oh Boy* and to the team at Red Hen Press for their work in editing, publishing, and promoting this book.

For time, space, and support: the University of Southern California and the University of Alabama.

To teachers and mentors at these universities and beyond. To friends and supporters too numerous to attempt listing, lest we leave someone out. Zachary held so many people in his heart and your support and kindness were deeply felt.

Most of all, thanks to his family Susan, Alan, Cody, and Jacob, who provided love and support throughout his journey.